Back To You This Christmas

S.L. STERLING

Dedicated to my sister, my best friend.
Thank you for always being there for me.

Earlier that year

While I sat waiting for the plane to board, I sipped on my coffee and fiddled with my phone. The airport was busy, as always, and I was on my way to my next photo shoot location. I had spent the last three years freelancing as a photographer and had traveled halfway around the world, visiting places like Paris, Italy, France, and Australia. It had been a wonderful experience, and at the young age of twenty-six, I had seen more of the world than people double my age. The traveling was amazing and part of the reason why I had gone into this line of work, but lately it wasn't enough; I felt something important was missing.

Those feelings began two days ago, while I was photographing this girl, Jasmine, on the day of her wedding with her mother. As I looked at them, laughing, through the lens of my camera, I began to miss home something terrible. Not only did I miss my parents, but I missed my bed, the sounds of the house, the homemade meals, everything. I had to put those feeling out of my mind in order to go on with rest of my day, being as happy and professional as I could, even though I was fighting back tears.

When I'd returned to my apartment that night, I was exhausted. I'd dropped my equipment to the floor and headed into the kitchen to make tea. However, it wasn't long before I found myself curled up on the kitchen floor crying my eyes out over everything that had happened over the last year. I'd hit a rough patch, and something had to change.

Eight months earlier, I had started dating my boss, something I had sworn I would never do, but he had been charming and relentless, so I had given in. Things had been going well, almost too well, and then what I feared the most happened. I had returned to the office after a rather rough day four weeks ago, and I'd found a letter addressed to me sitting on my desk. It was late, I was tired, so I shoved the envelope in my bag planning to read it at home. That had been a good plan on my part because inside the envelope, I'd found a letter explaining that things weren't working out between us and he thought it would better if we parted ways. We were over and I'd been fired.

For whatever reason, I hadn't been able to get the letter out of my mind. I'd wiped the tears from my cheek and blew my nose. I'd desperately needed to talk to my mother, so I'd pulled my phone from my pocket and dialed home. I'd needed to hear her voice and crossed my fingers that she was home, and she answered. I'd felt so defeated and wondered if maybe it was time I went home for a longer visit than my regular thirty-six-hour period.

Mom's voice finally broke through the other end of the phone. "Hey, sweetie, you're calling late." Then her voice quivered a little. "Everything okay?"

Shit, I had forgotten to do the time conversion before I called. It had to be eleven at night back at home.

"Everything is fine, Mom. Just really missing home," I answered quickly, sniffling and picking at my broken fingernail. I didn't blame her for worrying. I was her baby, off on the other side of the world, most of the time in the middle of nowhere, generally photographing animals and local people for magazine articles. Of course, she would worry when I made a call this late at night.

"Lexi you don't sound okay."

"Just a tough day, I guess. What's new?" I wanted to change the subject. I didn't want to focus on the troubles I'd had today. Hell, I still hadn't told her that I had broken up with Gary and that I'd been fired. I'd been holding out because I didn't want her to worry about me. She still didn't even know that I was working for someone else.

"Well, really, we are just getting ready for the wedding tomorrow."

"What wedding?" I asked, sniffling.

"Drew and Laura's. Your brother just got in tonight and they've gone out celebrating. I wish you could be here for this. I know Drew would have loved to have you there."

"Wow, really, already?" I glanced up to the calendar that hung on the wall and, sure enough, the large red heart I had drawn around the date stood out to me. I had received an invitation in the mail, but my bank account had ultimately decided for me that I couldn't go. I figured they would understand why I couldn't make it, and knowing Drew, he had probably sent me the invitation out of courtesy. He'd probably expected me not to be there. "I couldn't afford it, Mom."

"You should have said something. We would have paid for you to come home. We miss you, Lex."

"I know, Mom. I miss you guys too." I sniffled again. I got up off the floor and took a sip of my tea and pulled something to eat out of the fridge while listening to Mom talk about one of the neighbors. I took my plate of cheese and crackers over to the small table and sat down, picking up a pencil to write something down quickly.

"Oh, and your brother is coming home for Christmas this year," she said, changing the subject once again. "Would be nice if you could join us."

I fiddled with the pencil, holding back tears. I would give anything to sleep in my own bed, breathing in the familiar scent of Downy scented sheets. Right about now, I wanted nothing more than to taste one of her home-cooked meals and fresh-baked goodies too. I could barely cook, and I certainly couldn't bake. I stared down at my half-eaten cheese and crackers and pushed the food around on my plate while thinking about how close to heaven her food would be right about now.

"I know, Mom. Maybe next year."

We talked for another twenty minutes before I had to get off the phone with her. If I hadn't, I was sure the tears would start to fall as we talked about old times. I choked down my meal in silence, just like I had done most nights since I had been gone. When I put my dirty plate back in the kitchen, I turned and looked up at the calendar, that bright-red heart screaming at me. I let out a deep breath. She was so lucky to have him, I thought to myself and picked up the invitation that sat on the pile of mail on the table. These had to have been expensive, I thought to myself as I ran my fingers over the gold-leaf paper. Laura was so lucky. I threw the invitation down, took a couple of cookies from the bag on the counter, and my tea, and headed into the other room to watch some TV.

Fifty minutes later, the thought of home still hadn't left my mind, and I had begun checking out every airline for a flight home, finally booking one for December. I put it on my credit card, since my bank account certainly couldn't handle the cost of a flight right now, and decided that I would worry about it later.

As I sat waiting for the boarding call for my flight, I counted the weeks until I would be home—only twenty-six more weeks. I was so excited. This Christmas I would be sitting around the tree with my family for two weeks, instead of wallowing alone in misery.

Drew

June

"Today is the big day, man. You sure you're ready?" Zach looked over at me while tying his right shoe.

I was silent as I slid into my dress pants, pulling them over top of the black boxers with little red hearts that Laura had insisted we all wear for photos. I looked at myself in the mirror. Something about today was just surreal to me. It almost didn't feel real to be standing here getting ready for my wedding.

"Earth to Drew!"

I blinked hard and turned to look at Zach. I cleared

my throat. "Yeah, I guess. As ready as I'll ever be." I let out a sigh, looking at myself in the mirror again. I wondered how long it would be before I put on an extra forty-five pounds, said good-bye to my eight-pack that Laura loved so much, and replaced it with a beer gut.

"You guess? What the hell is that supposed to mean?"

I shrugged. I didn't know how to get what I was feeling across in words. Everything leading up to today had been wonderful, until I woke up this morning and something just hit. "Honestly, I don't know. Maybe I just woke up on the wrong side this morning." I looked over at my best friend who stood there smirking.

"Are you nervous?"

"No. I guess I'm just second-guessing if she is the one."

Zach was just about to reach for his shirt and stopped as the words left my mouth. "You're joking, right? Dude, you are getting married in less than an hour. Come on, she's a great girl. It's probably just cold feet. It will be fine."

I grabbed the perfectly pressed white shirt off the hanger and slid my arms into it. "I hope you're right."

Zach got up off the bed, walked over to the mirror, and tied his tie. "What do you mean you hope I'm right?

You've been with her for fifteen years, man. Of course, it's going to be fine."

"Yeah, but I should be ecstatic, happy, excited to start this journey with her, but instead I'm second-guessing everything. It's just a little unnerving."

"Seriously, man, it's just nerves. Breathe. It will be okay. You'll see her walk down that aisle looking absolutely stunning and you'll forget all about second-guessing."

I silently prayed Zach was right. However, he hadn't seen Laura's face when I dropped her off at her parents' last night. The way she hung onto me as she hugged me good-bye, or the tears in her eyes as she looked back over to me before I had left. I let out a breath and wrapped my tie around my neck when the other three guys came in carrying ten shots on a tray.

"Party time is here!" Ben yelled out, setting the tray down on the table in the middle of the room.

"What is that?" I asked as I finished tying my tie and adjusting my collar, adding the cufflinks to my sleeves.

"Tequila! Open up, motherfucker. You need to chill the fuck out!"

"Fuck, guys, Laura will kill me if she smells this on me. I can't. You guys go ahead. We made a promise to one another that there would be no alcohol before the ceremony."

"Already letting her control everything, are you? Don't be such a pussy!" Evan said, handing me the shot. "It's your fucking wedding, man. Drink it."

I chuckled at my seriousness and took the shot, praying that the smell would wear off before I stood across from her and said my vows.

"On three." Zach called one...two...and down went the shot. The hot, nasty-tasting liquid seared a path down my throat and heated my chest.

There was a constant murmur of voices that I soon blocked out as we continued to get ready. By the second shot, I noticed Zach looking over at me a couple of times, making eye contact, checking in to make sure I was indeed okay, but like the best friend he was, he never said a single word in front of the other guys. No one other than us knew how I was feeling.

A knock on the door quieted the guys down, and Zach quickly answered it. "Hey, Drew, boutonnieres are here!" I heard Zach yell as I stepped out of the bathroom.

I walked over, taking them from the guy at the door, and set them on the table. I stared down at the single red rose that Laura wanted us all to wear on our lapels and was overcome with that funny feeling again. I swallowed hard. Where was the damn wedding coordinator? She was supposed to be here already, and I feared if she didn't show up soon I was going to change my mind. Just as that thought ran through my mind, she appeared, almost as if she were the genie and I had just rubbed the magic lamp.

She came rushing in the door, grabbing everyone's attention. "Okay, boys, let's get these on, shall we." She grabbed one of the boutonnieres and began pinning it onto Zach.

I watched as she took turns pinning the flowers onto my three other friends before she turned to me. "All right, Drew, here we go. Are you ready?" she asked, carefully pinning the flower to my suit.

I nodded, swallowing my nerves down. "I just came from your bride's room. She looks stunning. Just wait until you see her." Once she had finished securing my boutonniere to my jacket, she quickly brushed a piece of lint away that had been sitting on my suit jacket and placed her hands on my chest. "All right, we should get down there."

I nodded, swallowing hard.

Minutes later, we were lined up at the alter, Drew on my left followed by the other three guys. I stood looking out at the guests, all 500 of them, and I started to sweat. I pulled at my collar, clearing my throat. "Did you remember the ring?" I whispered to Zach, who was busy making eyes at his girl, Ann Marie.

"Do you honestly think I would forget?" he, asked tapping his breast pocket. "Calm down, man, everything's going to be okay."

Seconds later, I saw the wedding coordinator peek her head through the doors at the back of the church and the "Wedding March" started to play as a deathly hush fell over the crowd and people stood. My nerves kicked into high gear as I waited for my bride to emerge through those doors.

Alexa

❧

December

I grabbed a large peppermint mocha from Starbucks and began walking toward my gate. I was so excited to be going home this year for Christmas. It seemed everyone was just as excited as I watched all the families getting ready for their flights to their holiday destinations. I took my time. I was at the airport early and took this opportunity to wander through all the overpriced shops, something I rarely had the time to do.

As I wandered through a purse shop, I thought back to this morning and the conversation I'd had with my landlord. I had packed everything I owned and had just thrown the last of my bags into the trunk of the cab and slammed it closed.

"Give me one minute," I'd said to the driver.

He nodded while sipping on his coffee. "I'm in no rush. The meter is running!" he shouted as I ran back into the building and handed the landlord my key.

"Alexa, are you sure you won't change your mind? I can always hold the place until I hear from you for no deposit. You've been a good tenant; I'd hate to see you go."

Of course, he would hate to see me go. I'd paid my rent on time, the place was barely used due to my travel schedule, and I had left it with barely a scratch in any of the walls or furniture.

I hesitated for a minute, trying to decide what my plan was. When nothing came to mind, I shook my head. "It's okay. I'm sure."

"You know what, you don't worry. I am going to hold it for you regardless. No one is going to be looking for an apartment over the holidays anyways. So, how about I call you just after Christmas, and if you want to come back, the place is yours."

"Thank you, I appreciate it, but you don't have to do that."

"Nonsense, it's not a big deal. It will be here for you. Have a merry Christmas, Alexa." He turned and headed

back down the hall in the direction he had come from. I wiped the tears that had fallen from my eyes and turned on my heel and walked out the door into the drizzly weather.

"Is there something I can help you with, miss?" I felt a light tap on my shoulder, and a lady came into focus in front of me.

"Oh no. I was just looking, thanks," I said and continued into the next store.

By the time I got to the gate, I had passed an hour. I took a seat off in the corner and pulled my laptop from my bag. Within minutes, I had pulled up job opportunities and began my search. There certainly wasn't much in the line of photography work back home, but the few that I found I applied to quickly. I had just sent my resume off to a fifth one when my cell phone rang. I glanced at the phone to see "Mom and Dad" across the screen.

"Hey, Mom."

"Lexi, I called your apartment. Your line has been disconnected."

"Yeah, Mom, I shut it off. Traveling to my next job," I lied. I hated lying to Mom, but she didn't need to know the real reason. I still really wanted my visit to be a surprise.

"Listen, I was just talking to your father. Are you

sure you can't make it home? We will pay for your ticket, even for a couple of days."

I looked around the airport and smirked to myself. "I can't, Mom."

The line went quiet, and I thought I heard her let out a sniffle, but then she cleared her throat. "So what time is your flight?"

"It leaves in three hours. Cell service might be spotty where I am going, but I will call you as soon as I can."

"How long is the flight?"

"About eleven hours."

"Where are you off to again?"

"Geez, Mom, I can't remember the name of the city, and I don't have my boarding pass just yet," I lied as I stared down at the boarding pass in my hand.

"All right, well, promise me you'll try to call us on Christmas day okay."

"Sure thing, Mom. I love you."

"Love you too, Lex."

The other end of the phone went quiet and I hung up, shoving it back in my bag. I stuffed my laptop and boarding pass in as well and pulled my sweatshirt from the bag. I threw it over my head and glanced across the way to the small store. Deciding I needed two or three books for the flight home, I got up from the floor and wandered across the way to browse what they had. Three hours later, armed with four new books, two bags of chips, a sandwich, and some other snacks and drinks, I boarded the plane and was on my way to spend Christmas with my family for the first time in three years.

A bad rendition of "Have Yourself a Merry Little Christmas" played over the tiny radio I kept in my office. The ice cubes in my now-empty glass had started to melt, sliding down one another and clinking against the side of the crystal glass. I poured a bit more scotch into my glass and looked out the window. Outside, snow was just starting to lightly fall, and the darkened skies threatened more.

I sat down and kicked my feet up on my desk, relaxing back in my chair. I picked up the paper that lay in front of me and stared down at the gold-leaf embossed invitation. They had only cost me a mere two thousand dollars to have printed—a bargain Laura had said, as she begged me to order them, and like an idiot, I'd complied. I read the written words over and over.

Drew John, Laura Elizabeth, on this first day of June, in holy matrimony - love that will last forever.

"Forever my ass," I said out loud as I threw the invitation down on my desk and picked up the glass, drinking down the remainder of my scotch. After fifteen years, it had all come to a grinding, crashing halt when the maid of honor was the last one to walk down the aisle. Laura, now known as the wedding wench, had left me, standing alone with my five groomsmen, in front of 500 of our closest friends and family, while she ran off with her new half.

I tell you nothing says fuck you more than having to hand over fifty grand in cash for your wedding that never happened. What I struggled to understand was why? How? How could my wife-to-be and girlfriend since college just up and walk away without an explanation and not feel the least bit heartbroken?

"Hey, Drew, I just wanted to stop in and make sure you were okay," Andrea said, stepping inside my office, glancing to the glass that I held in my hand.

She was one of the girls from the front desk who felt the need to constantly remind me of what had happened. Like everyone else, she always wanted to coddle me. We'd had a whole discussion one afternoon in the lunchroom. She firmly believed that I needed to talk to someone, that I was holding everything inside, but I wasn't. I was fine because, after a while, the hurt goes away, and all that was left now was a strong desire to know the truth.

"I'm good, Andrea. Thanks for asking." I was getting tired of this.

"Well, have a merry Christmas, Drew. If you are lonely at all over the holiday, give me a call. I decided to stay in town as opposed to going home to my family. Flights were crazy expensive last-minute. Perhaps we could share a coffee and desert one night."

There it was, her telltale "I can be a shoulder to cry on" offer. "Thanks for the offer, but I promised Zach I would spend the holidays with him and his family. So I'll be heading to Denver in the next couple of days."

I saw a flash of sadness in her eyes as she looked down to the floor. "Well, that is great, Drew. Have a merry Christmas." She stood inside my door, looking from me to the glass and back to me, almost as if she wanted to say something else.

"You too. You should get going before the weather gets any worse. Looks like there is going to be a good storm rolling in tonight." I nodded toward the window.

She smiled, turned, and slowly walked away from my office, looking back over her shoulder at me and giving me a tiny wave.

As soon as she was out of sight, I looked

around my office, the fake Christmas tree that stood in the corner with its flashing lights almost mocking me at the fact that this was my first Christmas alone in fifteen years. I turned my eyes back down to that stupid invitation and clenched my fists.

"Drew, could I see you for a second?" Trent asked, stepping inside the doorway of my dark office. "In my office please."

"Sure thing." I got up from my desk and followed him down the hall to his office, loosening my tie as I went.

"Shut the door behind you please," he murmured and took a seat behind his desk.

I did as he asked and sat down across from him. Something in me knew this was probably about the last few cases I had been working on.

"Drew, you are the youngest, highest paid divorce attorney in this firm. You have worked hard to get to where you are today. We are so proud of you and are hoping that you will stay on with this firm and become partner."

I just about jumped out of my seat. How great would it be to start the New Year as partner? But then he cleared his throat and continued.

"With that being said, you have fucked up. The last

two cases that you completed were disasters, both clients not happy with the outcome."

"Well then, I guess perhaps my clients should have thought about that before they stuck their dicks into someone other than their wives," I bit out.

Trent couldn't say anything to that. He knew me too well, and he knew my thoughts on cheating, especially after what had happened to me earlier this year. We both hated it, and having to represent someone who did it sometimes got to me. We'd had lengthy discussions surrounding the subject.

Trent let out a sigh and the corner of his mouth went up in a smirk. "Drew, one thing about you, you always say it like it is. Good thing we are behind closed doors and not in a boardroom full of other lawyers." He fiddled with the pen on his desk and deeply sighed before continuing. "Drew, the other partners and I are going to ask you to take some time off over the holidays. You've been working non-stop since, well, since June, and we think you might need a break."

I had nothing to say. This was just one more way that the wedding wench was going to screw me over, on top of the fifty grand I was still busy rebuilding in my investments.

"So starting Monday, I don't want to see you here until the New Year, and when you return, we all want that lovable, level-headed Drew that we used to know. Got it?"

I hung my head once again, feeling the weight of everything that had transpired six months ago. "Yes, sir." I placed my hands on his desk and stood up.

Since June, I had plowed myself into every case that had been thrown my way, never giving myself any downtime. I had worked morning, noon, and night, and pretty much every weekend just to avoid the thoughts of Laura and what could have been.

"What are you doing for the holidays, Drew?"

"I'm actually joining my best friend and his family in Denver for the holidays."

"Good, go home, Drew, spend time with family and friends. Give yourself a break and have a merry Christmas."

"You too, sir." I did my best to walk out of that office with my head held high, but it only worked for a short while until I found myself back behind my desk looking down at that fucking invitation.

I was beginning to think that this was going to haunt me for the rest of my life. I picked it up and threw it into my top desk drawer when my cell phone went off.

"Hello."

"Drew, it's Zach."

"What's up?"

"Not too much. Listen, I just landed in Denver and I'm heading up to the chalet tomorrow."

"Ah, well, have a safe drive! I'll see you when I get up there."

"No, not so fast. I figured I would pick you up on the way. Mom and Dad are expecting you."

"No, it's all right. I told you I would drive."

"Why, so you can sit and pine over what could have been for the next few days? No way. I'll see you tomorrow around one. You better be ready."

"No, man, don't bother. I'll drive up myself on Saturday."

Zach was already gone, and I was greeted with a dial tone as I spoke the last couple of words. I swore under my breath and pocketed my phone, grabbed my jacket and laptop, and made my way out of the office, shutting off the pathetic little plastic tree that sat in the corner before I left.

I stood and looked out my living room window, sipping on my coffee. Dark-gray clouds hung overhead, making the day appear gloomy. The storm that was supposed to hit last night was more than likely on its way today, and from the looks of it outside, it was going to be rolling in early.

I sat down on my couch and started scrolling through pictures on my cell phone, pictures I had sworn I would never look at again and didn't know why I hadn't deleted them yet. The same question rolled through my mind again: *How could she just walk away?*

After I had paid the wedding bill and said good-bye to our 500 friends, co-workers, and highly judgmental family while profusely apologizing for the lack of wedding celebration and fun, I had called her. To be honest, I wasn't expecting her to answer, but she surprised me when she did. She didn't even sound upset, didn't even apologize. Instead, she was short and matter of fact, as if we were nothing more than mere acquaintances. It was that moment that I realized I had no idea what had happened between us.

"Yo, Drew, you ready?" I heard the back door bang and Zach call from the kitchen.

"Jesus, man, you scared me half to death. I told you I would drive myself!" I called out from the couch, quickly shutting down the screen on my phone just in time for Zach to step around the corner. *I really should take my spare key back*, I thought to myself as Zach grabbed an apple from the bowl of fruit on the counter and took a bite.

"I know, but you are a lawyer, and lawyers lie. Where's your shit?"

"It's ready," I answered as Zach looked around the room for some sort of luggage.

"If it's ready then where is it?"

"God can't a man enjoy his Saturday morning coffee? Give me a minute and I'll get it," I said, getting up from the couch and heading toward my bedroom.

"I had my morning coffee three hours ago," Zach called out as I returned carrying my bag. "You're only taking one bag? I thought we'd hit the slopes while we were up there."

"Then I'll have to buy all new equipment. I sold all mine after..."

"For God's sake, man, she left. You're not dead. Single men can still ski, you know."

One thing about Zach I could always count on was that he didn't coddle people, especially me. Everyone around me wanted to wrap me up tight and protect me from all the hurt they thought I had going on inside. Zach, though, treated me just like he always did, because he knew the truth: I wasn't hurting, per say. I was just stumped more than anything.

"It's fine. I'll get new stuff up there."

Zach nodded and took another bite of the apple. "We should get on the road before the weather gets much worse. We have a good drive ahead of us."

"Yeah, yeah, give me a second to clean out the fridge." I walked into the kitchen, Zach following behind me. I pulled the garbage over to the fridge and signaled for him to hold the bag open as I began throwing stuff away that was sure to go bad before I returned.

"Man, I really would have thought all this would have been done before I got here," he said between the last few bites of his apple, throwing the core into the bag.

"And you said you would be here at one! Just relax, don't get your boxers in a bunch. You weren't even supposed to be here, remember? I was driving myself at one point." I laughed and dumped the remaining food into the garbage, tying the bag tight and pulling it from the can.

"Give me this. Go grab the rest of your shit," Zach said, pulling the bag from my hand and taking it out to the curb.

I hurried to set the timers on the living room lights

and pulled the blinds closed. Carrying my duffle bag, I locked the door behind me and walked over to Zach's rented SUV.

"Where the hell you get the granny mobile?" I laughed.

"Shut up and get in. You try renting a vehicle a few days before Christmas. You are guaranteed nothing of style, even with a reservation that you made four weeks in advance."

I laughed and hopped inside, glancing back at the house as he backed out of the driveway. Two weeks up in the mountains with people I had known my entire life, who treated me like family and never turned their back on me. I wouldn't lie, I was looking forward to it. If I came back with nothing but a rested body and mind, I would be okay with it, but what I really wanted this Christmas were answers.

I took my purse, leaving the remainder of my bags in the cab that was sitting in my parents' drive-way. I quietly climbed the stairs of the front porch and stood at the front door and rang the bell. I watched through the hole in the wreath as Mom came around the corner from the kitchen, wiping her hands on her red Christmas apron, stopping to adjust a blanket on the back of the couch before she even looked out the front door at who it was. As soon as her eyes landed on me, she ran to the door and ripped it open.

"Lexi, oh my God, Lexi." Mom threw her arms around me, hugging me tightly. "When...How did you get here?" she asked, letting me go, looking at me, and then pulling me back against her again.

"I took an Uber, Mom." I laughed as my face smashed against her shoulder as she pulled me in for yet another hug.

"An Uber? Lexi, you should have called. We would have come down to the airport and picked you up," she said, hugging me tighter.

"I know, but I wanted to surprise you." I laughed, hugging her back. "Are you surprised?"

"Jim. Jim, get down here," Mom called over her shoulder and pulled me in the house. "Of course, I'm surprised."

"Mom I need to get my bags," I said, trying to stop her.

"Nonsense, your father can get them. Jim..."

"For the love of God, woman, what is it?" Dad yelled as he ran up the stairs from the basement.

"Look who's home!"

Dad turned the corner and took one look at me. "Lexi! How's my girl?" he asked, pulling me in for a hug.

I leaned in and hugged him, taking in a whiff of his cologne—Old Spice. The familiar scent reminded me of when I was five years old and I would curl up on his lap every chance I got for story time. "I'm good, Dad," I said, hugging him tightly.

"Jim could you get Lexi's bags from the driveway?" Mom asked, sweeping me inside.

"Sure thing," he said, grabbing his boots from the closet, while I shuffled things around in my purse looking for my wallet.

"Here, Dad, money for the cab," I said, handing him a bunch of folded bills.

"No, no, I got it. Go in and get comfortable and put your money away," he said, throwing his coat on and running down the stairs to the cab that waited in the driveway.

Within minutes, Dad had all my belongings inside and was taking everything upstairs to my old room, Mom following behind me as I climbed the stairs with one of my small bags. I walked into my old bedroom; it looked exactly the same as it had the last time I had been home. I walked over and sat down on the double bed and picked up Mr. Wiggles, my most favorite teddy bear from when I was a kid.

"Mom, why do you still have Mr. Wiggles out?" I asked, letting out a laugh as I looked at the bear with a missing eye.

"Because it wouldn't be your room without him," she said, coming into the room carrying an extra blanket over her arm and laying it at the bottom of my bed.

"Thanks for the extra blanket," I said, setting Mr. Wiggles back down.

Dad set the suitcases down in the corner by the closet door. "What a wonderful Christmas present," he said, wrapping his arms around me again.

They both watched as I grabbed one of my bags and began emptying it and shoving clothes in my dresser drawers.

"All right, we are going to go downstairs and get dinner started. You get settled." Mom grabbed hold of me and kissed my forehead. "I cannot believe that you are actually here. Your father is right, what an amazing Christmas gift." She squeezed me hard and finally let me go and looked down at all my luggage on the floor. I could tell she wanted to ask about all the luggage I had brought, but she didn't say anything. She just quietly closed the door to my bedroom, Dad following behind her, and left me to unpack.

The next afternoon, I sat in the kitchen with a warm cup of hot chocolate in front of me while watching my mother roam around gathering ingredients for the next batch of cookies she planned to make.

"Did you want any mini marshmallows in that?" she held up a bag of the little multicolored marshmallows I loved.

"Sure."

She handed me the bag and continued searching the pantry for ingredients, placing the containers of cinnamon, nutmeg, and sugar down in front of me, then she began pouring ingredients into a bowl. It had always amazed me how my mother could bake. She made it look completely effortless. The woman very rarely used a recipe, often pulling the ingredients from some mental cookbook. I had no idea how she did it, but every single item she baked turned out perfectly. I certainly didn't have her talent. Not one thing I had ever tried to bake in my lifetime had turned out.

I dumped in a handful of marshmallows, stirred them into the hot liquid, Mom glancing at me every now and again.

"So, Lex, it's not that I'm not happy to have you home, but what gives?"

"What do you mean?" I asked, finishing topping off my mug with more marshmallows.

"Lexi, I'm not stupid. You brought all your bags home," she said, waving my grandmother's wooden spoon at me then stirring up the mixture in the bowl.

She claimed it was all because of that wooden spoon that everything turned out the way it did.

"Mom, you're acting as if I never come home. I was just here a few months ago."

Mom stopped what she was doing and looked at me, studying me, trying to read between the lines.

"Really, Mom, I'm fine. Everything is fine. I was just really missing home," I said, bringing the mug to my lips and sipping the now super-sweet chocolate marshmallow mixture.

"Lexi, you were home over thirteen months ago." Just as Mom went to say something else, the oven timer went off, signaling that the batch of cookies in the oven was finished, changing her train of thought. She bent down and removed the tray, then slid the cookies off onto a cooling rack before sliding the next sheet of cookies into the oven. The smell of chocolate chips filled the air, which made my mouth water. When she turned around to put more doughballs onto the baking sheet, I snagged one of the fresh hot cookies from the rack.

"Ouch," I let out as I inhaled a breath, the hot chocolate burning my fingers.

"Lex, careful, those are hot," Mom scolded as I bit into the hot, soft cookie. It fell from my hand onto the kitchen island, breaking into two pieces. I gave her the same smile I probably had when I was five after stealing hot cookies from the cooling rack. I picked up a piece of the cookie and popped it into my mouth. One thing I never had to worry about: Mom cleaned better than she cooked. That cookie could have fallen onto the floor and I would have eaten it.

"What are you making now?" I asked, nosing into the bowl in front of me.

"Sugar cut-outs," Mom said as she moved the cooling rack over by the stove, no doubt so I wouldn't eat all the cookies before they had cooled. "Want to pick out the cutters?" she asked, handing me the familiar dented and scratched red tin that she stored the cookie cutters in.

I lifted the lid and started searching through the tin for my favorite ones, while Mom started adding ingredients. "Oh, Mom, I could really use a new bed," I said, pulling out a Christmas tree-shaped cutter. The bed I had was old, and even though it held all the familiar dips in the mattress, it was much smaller than what I was used to.

Mom stopped what she was doing and looked at me and laughed. "Lex, whatever is up with you, promise me you will tell me when you know. As for a new bed, we'll see what we can do okay." She sighed, picking up that wooden spoon again and began stirring what would eventually become the sugar cutout batter.

"Mom...how many times must I tell you, nothing is wrong."

"I know my children, Lex. Something isn't right. I'm not going to pry or force you to tell me. So, just promise me that when you have figured it out, you'll share."

I ignored what my mother said, picked up the last piece of cookie from the counter, and popped it in my mouth as I continued picking out the cutters. Once I had the ones I wanted, I continued watching as Mom mixed in ingredients and stirred, every now and again checking on the cookies that were in the oven. How she knew something was up when I couldn't even explain what was going on with me was beyond me, but she did know her children, I would give her that.

Truth was, I didn't know why I had such a strong urge to come home. Perhaps it was because it was Christmas and my least favorite time of the year to be alone, or something greater had pulled me here which I had yet to understand. Whatever it was, I was content to be here.

The familiar sounds of the washing machine, the smell of the cinnamon, apple, cranberry concoction Mom had boiling on the stove to make the house smell more Christmassy, or the welcoming feeling of home as I stood in the driveway... Whatever it was, I was just happy to be sitting in the kitchen, drinking hot chocolate and eating the best warm chocolate chip cookies in the world.

Drew

"Hungry?" I asked, holding up a bag of sour cream and onion chips as Zach pulled the car from the gas station parking lot and back out onto the highway.

"Starving. Open those up."

I clicked my seatbelt into place first, and then peeled open the bag of chips. I took two chips and shoved them into my mouth before setting the bag in between us on the console. Zach reached in and took a couple as well, while I pulled back the tabs on the two cans of pop I had bought.

"How are things going at the firm?" I asked as I popped another chip in my mouth and wiped my hand on my jeans.

"Good, busy. You?"

"Busy. You know I'm glad that I told you I would come up for the holidays. I needed a break from all that shit." There was no way I was going to let on that the firm had agreed I needed holidays. "Mind if I turn up this song?"

"Go for it," he said, tapping his thumbs on the steering wheel as he drove.

I reached over and cranked the volume. I just wanted and needed to shut everything out for a while, and that was exactly what I planned to do.

"You realize this is the first time we have spent any time in length together since we took holidays in the spring, right?"

"Yeah, how could I forget? That was a great time. How's things with Ann Marie?" I asked as I drank down the remainder of my pop and shoved the can into the empty bag that sat at my feet.

"Couldn't be better, man. She'll be up with her family this week as well, and I believe she is coming to spend Christmas afternoon with us."

"That's great, man. It will be nice to see her again." I sat back, relaxing against the heated seat and thinking back to last spring break.

I had gone out to visit Drew and Ann Marie for a week by myself because Laura had to work. As the week went on, I remembered thinking to myself that their relationship was so different from ours. It was the little things: the way that Ann Marie touched Zach, the way they looked at one another in the quiet moments. I tried not to let it get to me and just chalked it up to the fact that the relationship was relatively new. However, thinking back now, our relationship hadn't ever been like that, even when we were first dating.

"Any more talk on a date yet?" I asked, looking out the window. The farther north we had driven, the more snow had accumulated on the roads, making them rather slippery.

"We agreed to set one after Christmas. She wanted to wait and get all the holiday stuff out of the way first."

"That's awesome. Hey, it looks like we may just be in luck for some good skiing weather," I said, digging my hand back into the bag of chips and shoving a couple into my mouth.

"Yeah, I'm pretty excited about it! Lots of snow in the forecast. Should be the best skiing season we've had in a while up here." He glanced over at me. "So, man, how are you really doing?"

I dropped my head in defeat and let out a loud sigh. "My God, not you too."

"What? You're my best friend. Am I not allowed to care?"

"You're allowed to care, but Lord, everyone around

me has been acting as if I am some tiny fragile human being, and I am not. I got left at the alter. It's not like she died."

"I know, man." Zach got quiet, and I suddenly felt bad for snapping at him. I knew his concern was genuine.

"Look, I'm sorry. I'm doing all right. I'm just getting tired of the pity, you know what I mean?"

Zach looked over to me, another question forming in his mind.

"Go ahead, ask away."

"Did you sense something was wrong between the two of you?"

I rolled my eyes. *Here we go.* "I don't know. I just remember watching you and Ann Marie last spring. Laura and I never had the type of relationship you guys have. Truth be told I was a little jealous of that. After that weekend I spent with you guys, I felt something was off between us but couldn't put my finger on it. We were both busy with wedding plans and figured we were just burned out from everything. However, she gave me no indication that she was unhappy. Hell, we were still having Sunday dinners with her parents up to a week before the wedding."

"What happened then?"

"If I knew, I would tell you," I said, shrugging my shoulders.

"You do know she's engaged already, right?"

I let out a sigh. "Yeah, I went to pick up a few of my things from her place a month or so ago. Her parents were there and they told me. I won't lie, it caught me a little off guard."

"How do you feel about her being engaged so soon?"

"Honestly?"

"Yes," he said, taking a sip of his pop.

"The only feeling I can describe is one of relief. It's like I told you the morning of the wedding, I should have been happy and excited to start my life with her, but I wasn't. Everyone told me it was just cold feet. Perhaps I wasn't the only one with cold feet."

"Maybe you are merely numb to it all. Maybe that is why you aren't upset about it."

I let out a laugh. "Nah, I don't think so. Maybe I'm still processing it, but to be honest, the only logical explanation I have is that I am my mother's child. That's it." I shrugged.

"Drew, you are nothing like her. Just because she walked out on your dad and you when you were younger and didn't act like she cared doesn't mean that you are the same."

"Sure it does. You explain it then." I shrugged.

"Okay, I don't think it's that at all. Perhaps you just haven't found the right woman yet."

"Zach, I had been with Laura for fifteen years. Fifteen years, man. We never fought, we liked all the same things, and we did everything together."

Zach held up his hand for me to stop. "Perhaps that is just it. Couples should argue, man. You should have an all-out fight occasionally, clear the air. It's not natural for people to get along one hundred percent of the time."

"True. Now can we please talk about something else?"

Zach put the blinker on and turned onto the familiar road. "You got it. You ready for my mom's apple raisin pie?"

I had spent many years with Zach and his family up here after my mom had left, my father having gone down a very bad road with alcohol addiction. They had become a second family to me, and it was to them that I owed for what I had today. If it hadn't been for their influence on me, I would probably be just like my dad, drunk on some street corner somewhere in the city.

"Honestly, I can't wait," I said, looking out the window as Zach drove into the main part of town.

Everything looked the same as it always did. We

drove past all the same little stores in the town center, most of them the ones that we used to visit during the summer holidays.

"How's Lex?" I asked.

"She's good, off freelancing around the world. She is such a flighty spirit. I have no idea how she does what she does. The girl has no guarantee of income, but somehow she manages to land on her feet every single time."

"That's great. We all should be more like her."

Zach looked over at me as if I had lost my mind. "You sure you're feeling all right?" He chuckled.

"Yeah, I'm good. I just figure she probably has a lot less stress than we do. We have responsibility." I laughed.

Zach pulled onto the familiar street and into the driveway of the family's home. The chalet looked the same as it always had, a mix of stone and wood front, the large picture window in the front overlooking the mountain behind us.

"Home sweet home," Zach whispered.

I looked up at the front of the house. The only decorations they had out were the wreath on the front door and the garland sprays on the railings. Two wreaths also hung off the outside lights. The rest, as usual, would be for us to put up. Zach and I would do the outdoor lights and the tree as always. As I looked up at the front door, a funny feeling sunk into the pit of my stomach, and I suddenly felt very out of place.

I hadn't even undone my seatbelt when Zach turned toward me, already standing outside of the vehicle. "Are you coming or are you spending the holidays out here in the driveway?"

"Man, perhaps I should just stay at a hotel," I mumbled.

Zach was just about to pull out a couple bags from the back seat but stopped what he was doing and looked at me. "You'd better be kidding. You know you are welcome here always. Hell, my mother would chase you all the way back to the city with a rolling pin if she heard you say that."

We both let out a laugh. "Yeah, hell, you're probably right."

"We should get inside. I know when I spoke to her the other day she said she was planning on baking up a storm yesterday and today. I also know for a fact that she has our favorite cookies in there right now, probably just cool enough to sneak in a few bites before dinner."

I remembered the cinnamon swirl cookies he was referring to and my stomach let out a growl. "Sounds great." I hopped out of the car and grabbed my bag from the back seat, giving Zach a hand with his bag as he grabbed his ski boots and helmet. We raced up the stairs just like we had when we were kids, Zach pushing me out of the way to get inside first, both of us laughing as I slipped on the icy step and dropped our bags, putting my hands out to brace myself from falling. I bent down to pick up the bags and Drew went to reach for the door handle.

"That's it, fuck face, the cookies are–"

Zach stopped mid-sentence. "Fuck you, they are," I said, laughing as I picked up the bags I had dropped and continued the climb up the stairs, running straight into Zach's back.

"What the hell are you two doing making all this noise. You both sound like a herd of elephants coming up those front stairs. You scared Mom and me half to death."

"What the hell are you doing here?" I heard Zach mutter as I came to a stop.

I didn't need to look around him to know who it was. I'd recognize that voice anywhere, and Zach had spoken the exact words that were running through my mind.

I stepped up beside Zach and looked at the brunette who stood before us. She wore a form-fitting white angora sweater and black leggings, her curves filling out both pieces of clothing perfectly. She had grown into quite a beautiful woman, and I couldn't help but allow my eyes to run over her a couple more times before her blue eyes sought mine.

What the hell was Lexi doing here?

"Alexa, what the hell are you doing here?"

I was just about to answer when I saw Drew come up behind my brother. Drew, the boy I'd had a crush on ever since he pushed my brother for acting like a total boy.

I was eight and we had all been playing on the playground one afternoon. Zach had decided that it would be fun to surprise me with a present. He had come over with his hands behind his back, Drew trailing behind shaking his head. He had told me to close my eyes and hold out my hand, claiming he'd found a special caterpillar he wanted to share with me. Being the naive younger sister who trusted her brother, I did as he asked. Only when he dropped the item into my hand

and told me to open my eyes, I was faced with a huge, slimy earthworm that slid and twisted in my hand.

I started screaming and crying, Zach started hysterically laughing, but Drew? Drew got angry. He shoved Zach hard onto the ground and told him to stop picking on me. From that day on, I had crushed on Drew something fierce, all through high school, college, and until the day I left home, but it didn't matter because to him I would always be Zach's little sister.

Stepping off to the side, I let the boys in. Zach stepped inside and placed his boots and helmet off to the side. He then grabbed me, wrapped me in his arms, and pulled me in for a big bear hug. Then he let me go, removed his jacket and boots, and stepped off to the side to allow Drew to come in.

"Hey, Drew." I waved awkwardly, looking into his blue eyes.

"Hey, Lexi." He held his arms open for a hug.

At first, we awkwardly bobbed and weaved, and then I stepped into his arms and he wrapped them around me, pulling me in close. I expected a quick hug, but instead he surprised me by holding me tight for a little longer. I couldn't help but inhale his scent as I buried my face into the crook of his neck.

"Welcome home, boys!" Mom called out from

behind us. Drew instantly let me go to greet my mother and father.

As I watched my mother and then my father greet both of the boys, a sense of peace came over me. Something about being home at this time of year warmed my heart. I was glad that I had decided to come home for two weeks and spend Christmas with everyone.

"You boys are just in time for dinner! Roast beef, potatoes, vegetables, how does all that sound?" Mom asked, taking Drew's coat from him and fixing the collar of his shirt, something she had always done when he was growing up. Then she placed her arm around Drew and walked with him upstairs and into the dining room.

I stepped out onto the front porch as the boys followed my parents to the kitchen and pulled their bags inside. Then I leaned against the door and locked it. I closed my eyes for a second and inhaled deeply, looking up into the dining room. I watched as Drew sat down, smiling at my mother as she handed him the bowl of mashed potatoes. He really had it all: looks, body, brain, and a kind heart.

"Lexi, are you coming?" my mother called out, looking rather impatient. "We would like to eat."

"Yes, Mom, I'm coming." I walked up the stairs and over to the table while staring at Drew. However, there was no use in wanting what I couldn't have. It was a dead-end road with him, I already knew that.

I flopped down in my usual seat, which happened to be beside Drew, and waited until Zach passed me a bowl of vegetables.

All through dinner, Dad basically grilled Zach and Drew on some of the legal happenings that were going on in the world. I was pretty much oblivious to all of them. That's what happens when you live in another part of the world—you become disconnected from everything—but I listened intently and practically hung onto every word Drew said.

Drew

I sipped on a cup of coffee and took a bite of the huge slice of apple pie that sat in front of me. I had really missed having home-cooked meals and family to eat them with. Normally for me it was whatever I could whip up quickly after a long day and generally involved a microwave while looking over legal documents. However, I knew that these two weeks would be filled with amazing homemade meals, wonderful desserts, and feeling like I once again belonged somewhere.

I was thankful that during dinner tonight no one asked about Laura. Even though I knew they would have my best interest at heart, I really didn't care to talk about her. Plus, it had been nice to be able to forget about her and not be coddled by family, even though I would have preferred if anyone were to do it, it be them. I relaxed back against my seat, taking another bite.

"Anyone want any more coffee?" Barbara asked, coming over with a fresh pot.

"I'd love to, but I can't. I have to meet Ann Marie tonight," Zach announced and glanced at his watch. "And it's already close to seven, which means I'll be late if I don't get ready and leave in fifteen." Zach drank down the remainder of the coffee in his mug and got up from the table, taking his bag to the basement, to his old room to get ready.

"Well, I have nowhere I need to be, so I'll have another one please," I said, placing my mug near the edge of the table and smiling.

"Sure thing, dear," Barbara said, filling my mug along with Lexi's and returning the pot to the coffee maker.

"Okay, kids, same rules apply. Lexi, you and Drew are on dish duty tonight. Tomorrow it will be Zach's turn. I think we are going to retire for the evening. We'll be in the basement watching TV if you need us," Barbara said, leaning against the back of her chair and smiling over at her husband. "Good night," she said, leaning down and giving Lexi a kiss on the top of her head, doing the same to me as she walked by.

"Night," we both said in unison, watching after them as they left.

I glanced across the table at Lexi. She sat there, her hands wrapped around her mug, sipping away on her coffee, swirling her fork through the leftover apple pie on her plate, when her eyes met mine. She smiled softly and cleared her throat, looking back down to the cup in front of her.

Almost instantly, she got up and began clearing the plates, scraping each of them into the garbage and setting the silverware in the sink. I was just about to start helping when I felt her hand on my shoulder.

"It's fine. Relax, drink your coffee. I'm just going to get some things soaking."

I watched as she cleared the entire table, putting leftover food away into containers and neatly piling the dirty plates on top of one another.

After I had finished the last of my coffee, I wandered into the kitchen with my mug in hand. She was standing by the sink, hot water steaming in front of her. I couldn't help but check out her perfect figure. She was placing more silverware and cups into the hot water.

"You wash, I'll dry?" I suggested, leaning up against the counter, studying her face as I held out my mug for her to take.

"Sure, Drew, sounds good." The smile that danced

on her lips as her eyes met mine made me smile inside.

I reached around her and grabbed the towel that she had gotten out for me and waited until the first few glasses and mugs were ready to dry. We worked in silence beside one another just like we always had. Occasionally, I would catch her sneaking a glance at me, her full pouty lips turned up into a half-smile as her eyes meant mine, but she continued to wash the dishes, placing them down for me to dry.

"Would you mind turning on the radio?" she asked, swallowing hard, almost as if the silence between us was too uncomfortable for her. "I feel like listening to some Christmas music."

"Sure thing," I answered and leaned over, flipping the power on the little radio, Christmas music instantly filling the room. "That was easy. Didn't even need to find the station." We both laughed.

We had washed every dish in silence, and once she had put the roasting pan in to soak, she removed her gloves, turned toward me, and stood leaning up against the sink, her arms crossed beneath her breasts. I couldn't help but check her out a little bit more than I had when I first arrived. She had grown up since the last time I had seen her. She had filled out and had become a woman—a rather attractive woman.

I looked down as she placed her hand on my forearm, a strange tingle running through me.

"Drew, I wanted to say that I'm sorry I couldn't make it to your wedding. I really wanted to be there," she said, making eye contact with me again.

"It's okay. You didn't miss very much." I shrugged, laying the towel down on the counter. "Just ask your brother."

"He told me what happened. I'm so sorry."

I shrugged. I didn't want her sympathy. I didn't want people, especially Lexi, looking at me like...like they all had been for months. "So, Zach told me that you had a project in Paris over that time. That's must have been exciting," I said, changing the subject.

"Yes, I was doing a fun shoot for a lingerie campaign."

"That's awesome. Did it go well?"

"It paid the bills for a couple of months. That's all I really wanted." She shrugged and put the rubber gloves back on to wash the last of the dishes.

"Where are you living now?" I asked, while I dried the last dish. She pulled out a bottle of cleaner and wiped down the counters.

"I was renting a little place over in Italy. A cute one-bedroom. It was near this amazing pastry shop."

"Nice. It's beautiful over there," I said, sitting down at the island and watching her make her way around the kitchen, finally finishing and hanging up the wet towels to dry.

"I didn't know that you've been to Italy." She poured us each another cup of coffee and sat down beside me.

"Yeah, well, it was with Laura, so...I tend not to talk too much about that part of my life." I smiled. "Perhaps one day I will go back."

She grew quiet. I hadn't meant to make her feel bad. It was just a fact of life. It was a better part of my life that right now I didn't want to revisit in any capacity, especially if I was going to have a good Christmas.

"What are you planning to do tomorrow?"

"Mom would really like us to get the Christmas tree tomorrow. You think you'd be up for that? Zach already told me he would be off with Ann Marie."

"Sure. Sounds like fun."

She took a sip of her coffee, avoiding my eyes.

"I'd like to leave early. It's been forever since I walked around the town. Would that be okay with you? We could spend the day together."

"I'd love that. All right then, it's a date..." I could see the realization of what she had said in her eyes as they widened and her cheeks turned this cute shade of pink. "I mean, not a...not a date..."

"It's okay, I knew what you meant. Just let me know

when you're wanting to leave okay?" I winked at her and gently nudged her shoulder with mine to let her know that everything was okay.

She leaned into me, nudging me back, smiling up at me. "Sure thing. It's getting late. I should show you to your room. I'm sure you've had a long day."

"I have. I'm pretty tired." I nodded.

She picked up our mugs and ran them under the hot water, rinsing them both and leaving them in the sink. She shut the lights off in the kitchen and turned to me and smiled. "Ready?"

I nodded my head and followed her into the living room. She shut off one light beside the couch, leaving one on for Zach, and quickly shut the blinds and locked the front door. She started climbing the stairs as I grabbed my bag and followed her. I watched her hips sway back and forth in my face as she ascended, looking down to my feet as I felt my cock start to stir in my pants.

"I hope you don't mind sharing a bathroom with me?" She giggled as she walked over to the bedroom door across from hers and pushed it open, turning to smile at me. "It will just be like when you used to stay over."

"Great, you were always a bathroom hog. Shall we set up a schedule now or later?"

I shoved the door open and flipped the switch just inside the door to light up the room. This was one of my favorite rooms in the house because the bay window against the far wall overlooked the mountains.

"Here you go, this is your room. I got it all cleaned up for you today. Fresh sheets on the bed and two extra blankets for you in case you get cold," I said, stopping just inside the door.

"Extra blankets probably won't be necessary. I'm like a furnace," Drew said as he walked by me, his arm accidentally brushing against my chest as he walked by. The contact of his arm caused a shiver to run through my body and our eyes instantly locked. "Sorry about that," he murmured as he walked over to the bed and placed his bag down. "Does this work?" he asked, walking over to the TV on top of the dresser.

"It's okay, and yes, it works. I checked it out this morning," I said, nervously walking over to the lamp on the desk and turning it on.

"This will be perfect, thanks." He bent and turned the light on that was beside the bed.

I couldn't help but check out his ass as he did that. I swallowed hard when I caught a tiny peek at his bare skin as his sweater rode up his side.

"Towels are in the closet outside of the bathroom, and if you need anything at all, my room is just across the hall," I said, pointing to the open door across the hall.

"I remember where your room is," he winked at me. "Thanks." He turned and unzipped his bag, pulling out a pair of sleep pants and placing them on the bed.

I swallowed hard. He remembered where my room was. A giddy feeling built inside of me. "All right, well, I guess I will go and turn in." I didn't know why I was hesitating; I didn't have anything else I wanted say. Perhaps I just wanted to stand here and stare at him for a bit longer.

"Good night," he said, continuing to unpack some

things from his bag. Then he reached behind him and pulled his shirt off.

I felt my mouth start to water at the sight of his strong, broad shoulders and muscular back. He turned and caught my gaze as my eyes washed over him.

"Good night," I murmured, swallowing hard. I pulled his bedroom door closed and rushed across the hall into my room, silently closing the door and leaning up against it. Letting the coolness of the wood rest against my hot body, I took in a few deep breaths.

"Jesus get a hold of yourself, Lexi," I muttered. "You are a grown woman, not some lovesick teenager," I mumbled. "It's not like you haven't seen a naked man before." It just wasn't Drew.

I stood against the door for a few more minutes, and then pulled the door open with shaking hands and made my way to the bathroom to wash my face. Returning to my room, I pulled one of my favorite T-shirts and a pair of panties from the dresser drawer, got changed, and crawled into bed. Once I was tucked under the covers, I flipped the bedside light on and grabbed my book from my night table and began to read. I was soon lost in my book, until half an hour later a toilet flush took my mind from my book and brought me back to thoughts of Drew.

Drew all alone across the hall.

I dropped the book against my chest and thought about how it would feel to run my hands up his back and over his strong shoulders.

I was still awake at two in the morning. I was now lying in the dark, staring up at the ceiling. I had heard Zach come in around twelve-thirty and heard Mom and Dad come up to bed shortly after that. The house was now quiet, except for the sound of Dad snoring off in the distance. I lay in the warmth of my bed, my mind still reeling with thoughts of Drew, alone, across the hall. Drew had everything: good looks, a great job, he was successful, and for the life of me I couldn't figure out why some girl who'd had him would ever let him go. I'd give anything for a chance with a guy like him. Well, not just any guy, and here she was just throwing him away as if he were last night's trash.

I rolled over onto my side and let out a sigh. I needed to get my mind off him, and knowing he was right across the hall wasn't helping. The first thought that came to my mind as I rolled back over and stared up at the ceiling was cake. Mom had a coconut cream cake downstairs in the fridge, and the more I thought of it, the more I wanted a piece.

Finally, the craving won and I got up, threw on a pair of socks, and slipped out of my room. The house was silent, and I tiptoed down the stairs, carefully avoiding the creaky steps. I could see a tiny light that we always left on in the kitchen. I came around the corner to see Drew, shirtless, his sleep pants hung low on his hips, standing with his back to me. He hadn't seen me, or so I thought, and I was about to scurry back up the steps when he spoke.

"Hey, you want some cake?" he asked, holding out a plate with a slice on it. I came slowly around the corner, my eyes firmly planted on his chest and abs. Fuck. The man looked like one of the lingerie models I had photographed. He was so cut and well-defined. When my eyes met his, I saw him take a quick glance down my body, and that was when I realized I was in nothing but a short T-shirt and panties.

"Couldn't sleep?" I asked, taking the plate from his hand. My fingers brushed his, the contact sending a jolt through my body.

"No, and I couldn't get the thought of cake out of

my mind either. Your mom makes damn good cake, and this one just happens to be my favorite," Drew said, watching as I tried to hide my half-naked body behind the counter, a half-smile coming to his lips.

"What's so funny?" I asked as he turned and cut another slice of cake, placing it on another plate.

He turned around with fork in hand and dug into the soft, moist cake. He leaned up against the counter, his eyes roaming what he could see of my body as he ate. "I just think that it's cute that you are trying to hide from me. Especially when you don't need to hide from me, Lexi. I've known you pretty much your entire life. I've seen you in less clothing than that. We spent many summers all together by the pool."

I felt a blush rise to my cheeks. "I'm not hiding. I just wasn't expecting anybody to be up at this time. Besides, I'm not exactly dressed for a friendly chat. You've known me all your life, with clothes on," I said, nervously laughing, and stepped around the corner of the island, setting my plate down.

"So, look at me!" he exclaimed, holding his hands out to the side like he was putting himself on display. "Do I look like I'm dressed for a friendly chat?"

"Yeah, look at you, Mr. Eight-Pack." I rolled my eyes. "Do you want some milk?" I asked, holding the corner of my shirt down and raising my arm up into the cupboard for a glass.

"Sure."

I could feel his eyes burning into me as I reached for another glass and got the milk out of the fridge. I quickly poured two glasses and turned around, only to see him still staring at me. I did my best to ignore it and slid his glass over to him, returning to my slice of cake. I tried hard to avoid eye contact with him, but it was almost impossible, and when I checked him out again, I could see the outline of his semi-rigid cock through his sleep pants. I bit my lower lip and ate the last bite of the cake on my plate. Drew was already done with his and had put his plate into the sink. I walked over and put my plate in the sink on top of his while he put the cake back into the fridge.

I was about to turn around to grab his glass when I felt the heat of his body against my back. I could barely breathe and was afraid to move, so I grabbed the dish-cloth, preparing to wash up the dishes we had used. I turned toward the sink and was just about to turn the water on when I felt his fingers dance along the edge of my panty-line. Drew was touching me. Drew, the same boy who used to pick on me, was now standing behind me, a man, running his fingers against my bare skin. His touch was almost paralyzing as I struggled to breathe. He was so close to me that I could feel the light puff of his breath on the back of my neck. I could feel myself get instantly wet, and I bit my lower lip and closed my eyes as his fingers tickled along the side of my belly to grip the edge of my T-shirt and pull it down to cover over my ass.

As soon as I was covered, he leaned in, his scent intoxicating, and whispered in my ear, "Thanks for the cake. Good night, Lexi."

I closed my eyes. His hands were still grazing my skin, and I stood there allowing the room to spin around me. His hands then went to my hips and rested there for a couple of seconds, his warm touch searing into my skin, and then, as quickly as he was there, he was gone. The heat from his touch was gone. I turned around. He hadn't gone far; he was leaning against the other counter across from me, intensely watching me. I looked into his eyes and caught a glimpse of what I was sure was want.

At first, the look scared me a little because, well, this was Drew. He then stepped closer to me, the close-ness of his body making my nipples harden. I watched his eyes leave mine and look down at my lips, the silence around us almost deafening. I was almost sure he was going to lean in and kiss me, but the sound of the house settling caused him to back away.

Without saying a word, he left the kitchen and made his way back upstairs to his bedroom, leaving me alone in the dim light of the kitchen.

Drew

I lay on my side and stared at the clock. It was only 6:30 A.M. I had barely slept after coming back to bed last night. My dick was harder than steel, harder than it had been in a very long while. I was kind of relieved that it still worked, to be honest. The thoughts of Lexi standing at the counter in nothing but a T-shirt and panties certainly weren't helping matters. Why had I gone downstairs to have that damn cake?

I rolled over and flung my arm over my eyes and lay there thinking about last night. The images flashed through my mind at a rampant pace. Lexi, braless under the T-shirt she wore, her nipples hard enough to poke through the material, teasing me. How cute she had been trying to cover her sexy, rounded ass framed in those black cotton panties as she reached up to grab two glasses from the cupboard. That ass that at one point... I wished I could just bend her over the counter and do very nasty things to it. The same counter where she had baked cookies with her mother her entire life. Surely, I was going to Hell for those thoughts.

I let out a sigh and grabbed my cock, squeezing the base of it. The throbbing and ache it was producing was killing me. Maybe staying here really wasn't such a good idea. I mean, Zach hadn't expected Lexi to be here when he had asked me to join the family. I certainly didn't need another encounter with her like the one I had last night, or I was sure to have a raging case of blue balls this entire holiday season. Perhaps I should just call up one of the local hotels and go there instead. Sure, Barbara and Jim would be upset, but they would be more upset if they found me balls deep in their daughter.

I heard the clinking of dishes downstairs and decided I should probably get up or I risked missing breakfast. I quickly took care of my raging hard-on then slipped out of my sleep pants and into a pair of my favorite jeans and a sweater and made my way across the hall to the bathroom. I was just about to enter the closed door when I heard Lexi shout out, "Be out in a minute."

That would have been the last thing I'd need, to

walk in on her while she was in the shower, especially with her parents right downstairs. I closed my eyes, bit my lip, and turned to walk back across the hall when the door to the bathroom opened and Lexi stepped out into the hallway.

My heart started hammering in my chest as she was wrapped in a large green towel, her hair still wet from the shower. She looked sexy as hell as she stood there, her hair all tousled to the side.

"Good morning," she sang, resting her hand on my chest and patting. "Hope you slept well. Mom has fresh waffles downstairs. You should head down before Zach eats them all. I'll be down as soon as I get dressed and I get my hair dried."

I didn't say a word. She took her hand from my chest and walked off and slipped into her bedroom, closing the door behind her. I stood staring at her closed bedroom door, and the only thought on my mind was following her and devouring her on the other side of the door.

I finally tore my gaze away from her bedroom door and went into the bathroom, locking the door behind me. I started the shower and hopped in. There was no way I could go down to breakfast, not with a hard-on like I had, so I quickly snapped another one off in the shower.

Twenty minutes later, I made my way downstairs. Barbara had just refilled the plate in the center of the table with fresh blueberry waffles. Lexi sat beside her brother with three waffles on her plate, loaded with syrup. Between Zach and me, we devoured the last five waffles on the plate.

"Goodness, do you guys think you will want more waffles?" Barbara asked as she watched us devour the plate she had just made.

"I'm good, Mom," Lexi and Zach said in unison.

"Drew?"

"Plenty for me," I answered, pouring a fresh cup of coffee and passing the pot to Lexi.

"Did you want some syrup?" Lexi asked, holding up the bottle of syrup for me to take.

"Thanks." I took the bottle and drizzled the sticky brown liquid on my waffles. I passed the jug to Zach, who sat at the head of the table reading the morning paper and drinking coffee.

"How was your night with the lovely Ann Marie?" I asked.

"Amazing as always. We went downtown and hung around the large fireplace in the square. Did a little Christmas shopping, had a coffee and some cake, and then returned to her parents' for a movie. What about you? What did you do last night?"

Lexi's eyes flew to mine, a look of nervousness on her face, for fear I mentioned the cake incident. I winked at her and then answered Zach. "I did dishes with your sister and then hit the sack," I said, shoving a forkful of food into my mouth.

"You went to bed at what, eight o'clock? What are you, ten?" He chuckled.

"Shut up! I was tired okay." Lexi let out a little giggle. "Are you coming with us today to get a tree?" I asked, looking over at Lexi, watching as she licked syrup off her fingers and then quickly got up, excusing herself from the table, and went upstairs. I watched after her, praying that Zach would answer that he would be joining us. However, my prayers were soon crushed.

"No, sorry, man, I can't. Going skiing with Ann Marie and her parents. I promised her I would be there, so I can't exactly back out. Which reminds me, I should probably head over to her place shortly. Do you need anything out of the car before I go?" he asked as he glanced at his watch.

"No, I'm pretty sure I took everything out last night," I said, sipping on my coffee.

"All right then, guess I'll see you tonight?"

"I'll be here. Oh, could you pass me the paper before you go?"

Zach turned and whipped the paper at me, laughing as he took his plate to the sink and went on his way, leaving me in peace to finish my breakfast.

"Zach, don't forget we are decorating the tree tonight," Barbara said, turning to look over at us from where she was working away in the kitchen.

"No worries, Mom, I'll be here. See you later."

"Who got into my coconut cream cake?" Barbara cried when she opened the fridge door for something. "That was supposed to be for the charity gala!"

"Sorry, that was Lexi and me." I cleared my throat as Zach looked over at me, a strange look on his face.

"I should have known. You two always loved that cake. Have your fill. I'll make another one today." She laughed.

Zach had been gone for over a half an hour, and I was just finishing up the business section, drinking the last bit of my now cold coffee, when Lexi came bounding down the stairs, calling my name.

I turned to see her enter the kitchen. She had changed and now wore a long white sweater over black leggings. "You almost ready to go? Thought we could get into town and check out some shops before it gets too busy."

"Ready whenever you are."

"Dad said we could take his truck to get the tree."

"That will help." I laughed. "I'll drive." I threw the paper on the table and began clearing my dishes, and then I went over to the door and put my boots on. Lexi followed behind, slipping her feet into her knee-high black boots that hugged her legs perfectly.

"You don't mind if I take some photos along the way do you? I want to capture the snow and some decorations around town, maybe even some families down at the tree farm."

"Not at all, Lex."

Soon we were bundled into her father's truck and on our way down to the town center. We traveled in silence for a while, Lexi looking out the window almost as if she were afraid to look at me.

"Okay, so what are we getting?"

"Dad said he really wants a Fraser fir this year."

"Okay. No problem. I think we can handle that. Don't you?"

She nodded her head but still wouldn't look my way. I turned the radio up when *Allan Jackson's* "Let it Be Christmas" came onto the radio. I couldn't help but glance over at Lexi as she started humming along and then finally breaking into song. Her voice was pure heaven to listen to, always had been. I remembered when she had been the lead in the church choir one Christmas. She thought she sounded awful, but I could have listened to her sing forever, and I tried to assure her of that, but she didn't believe me.

"Do you remember the year you were head of the choir at the church?" I asked.

"Oh God, don't remind me! That was awful. I sounded horrid."

"No, you didn't. Out of all the Christmas performances I have been to with your family, you were by far the best."

"Ha-ha, then you, my friend, are completely deaf." She giggled, going back to looking out the window.

I smiled to myself at her response. That was Lexi, always afraid to admit that she was good at something.

"So tell me, where was your most interesting shoot done this year?" I asked as I continued driving down the snow-covered road.

Lexi had always amazed me. When she said she was going to freelance for a year or two, we all figured that she would be home within three months; however, she had succeeded, getting constant contracts and being able to make ends meet without once having to call her parents or brother for help. She had what it took to succeed, along with the drive and passion to go out and look for it when things weren't coming her way. I admired that about her. Most people would take the easy road and get out.

"Honestly, it won't be what you think. It would have to be the time I spent in Rome doing architecture photos for a travel magazine. Just getting to tour around the city, look at amazing and beautiful things, and admire them through my camera lens. It's indescribable."

Soon I was lost in her words. She had always had a way of filling quiet time with amazing stories.

I pulled the truck into the town square and parked near the tree lot, both of us climbing out of the truck. She met me around the front of the vehicle. "I figured maybe we could grab a hot chocolate and take a walk around before getting a tree."

"Perfect. I'd love that," she grumbled. She was trying to get the strap of her camera over the hood of her jacket, which kept getting stuck.

"Here, let me." I reached around behind her and pulled her soft, long hair out of the way and fixed the strap under her hood. Her eyes rose to meet mine. We stared at one another for a minute, neither saying anything, and then I cleared my throat and rested her hair on her shoulder. "We should go get that hot chocolate."

Her lips parted slightly, and she nodded her head as she continued staring into my eyes. I had to look away. I could feel the pull of her stare and knew if I didn't turn away now, there would be no turning away.

We walked over to the little diner on the corner. I opened the door and held it for her as she slipped inside. I walked over to the counter and ordered us each a hot chocolate, marshmallows loaded into hers, while she used the washroom.

"Here you go!" I held out the cup of hot chocolate to Lex as she came out of the washroom.

"Thank you." Taking a sip, her eyes lit up. "You remembered!"

I winked. "How could I have forgotten! You'd steal those marshmallows from me every single time."

"Well, that is only because I knew you didn't really like them," she said, nudging into my shoulder with hers.

"Well, that is true. What do you say we get going?"

We had spent the afternoon wandering around town, in and out of stores, stopping to look up at the ski hills and watch as people made their way down. I watched as Lexi took pictures, her creative spark ignited when she was behind the lens of her camera. She had finally dropped the camera and looked over at me, smiling.

"We should probably make our way back to the tree lot and pick a tree before they close," she put the lens cap on her camera and then placed the camera into her bag.

"Yeah, you're probably right. Your mother won't be very happy with us if we don't come home with a tree will she?" I said, gently bumping her shoulder. I really hadn't wanted today to end; I had enjoyed walking, taking in the sights of the town, and just being with Lexi. "Would you ever come back to the area? You really seem to love it here," I asked the question that had been burning in my mind all afternoon as I had watched her.

She pulled her gloves from her pocket and slid her hands into them, tilting her head in a thoughtful way. She shrugged. "I guess it would depend."

"On?"

"If I had a good reason to or not."

I couldn't help but stare at the look in her eyes as

the words fell from her lips. There was something up with her, and I bit my tongue and struggled not to ask her. I was about to say something when she grabbed my arm.

"Come on, let's get in there before they close up for the night," She began pulling me across the street toward the tree lot. Their business hours posted on their sign indicated they would be closing in an hour.

We began wandering the lot looking for the perfect tree—too short, too skimpy, too tall, too fat, not fat enough, needles falling off, the list went on and on. Thirty minutes later, she yelled over to me as I searched again through the Fraser section.

"I think I found it, Drew. Come look."

I walked through the mess of trees I had been sifting through when she came into sight, holding up a tree, a large grin on her face. "Isn't it perfect!" she exclaimed.

I shook my head. It certainly was perfect. Not too big or too tall, perfectly shaped, and so was the girl who was holding it.

"I think it's perfect," I said smiling at her, only I wasn't really talking about the tree. When I saw her start to struggle with it, I grabbed the tree by the trunk, taking it from her. I paid for the tree and threw it into the back of the truck, then I walked around to Lexi's door and opened it for her, helping her get in. I pulled the buckle across her lap and adjusted the strap across her chest as she looked into my eyes, the click of the belt lock sounding loudly through the truck. This was going to be a perfect Christmas.

We pulled into the driveway in time to see Zach walk out of the garage. He walked over to the car and pulled his skis from the trunk and carried them back into the garage. Drew put the car in park, and I hopped out.

"I'll go in and get the decorations down from the storage room; you guys bring the tree inside!" I shouted as I ran up the front steps to the house.

"Alexa don't slam the door," I heard Mom call from the kitchen.

"Mom, wait until you see it. It's perfect!" I exclaimed, placing the stand on the floor in the living room—the same spot the tree had gone in since I had been a child, right in the front room window. I had always loved coming home from school and seeing the tree, its lights flashing to the world as I climbed up the front steps. As I would walk through the door, the warm scents of cinnamon and nutmeg greeted me just like they had today. It was as if I had been transported back through time.

The first thing I did was flip on the radio to the all-day Christmas station and grab the step stool from the closet just as the front door opened. Drew came in carrying the trunk of the tree, with Zach trailing behind holding the top. They were both laughing as they tried to maneuver the tree up the stairs and into the sitting room.

I climbed on the stool and pulled down the boxes from the top of the storage area, setting them one by one on the table. I couldn't help but giggle as I listened to Zach and Drew as they continued to struggle to get the tree set up.

"Zach, since you were absolutely no help, as always, why don't you get down on the floor and help me guide this baby into the stand."

"Why? Has it been so long you're afraid you won't be able to find the hole?" Zach broke out in fits of laughter, dropping the top of the tree onto the floor as Dad smacked him across the back of the head.

"That is enough of that wiseass," Dad scolded. "You

may be an adult, but remember you're not too old to get a smack."

Drew started to laugh as he picked up the tree and stood it upright, being careful not to set the trunk down on the white carpet.

I felt my cheeks redden at the comment Zach had made to Drew but did my best to pretend I hadn't heard a word he had said. Mom came in carrying a tray full of hot apple cider and set it down on the living room table. The hot apple cider was a tradition when we decorated the tree, and so was the cinnamon stick that sat in each of the mugs.

Mom took one look at me and instantly her hand went to my forehead. "Lexi, honey, you are feeling all right. You look flushed."

"I'm good, Mom."

She dropped her hand and looked at me, but I just continued pulling open the box of decorations. I began sifting through them, trying to keep my eyes from wandering over to Drew, who now had his coat off and was adjusting the tree, while Zach lay on the floor shouting out instructions. I glanced up again and watched the muscles in his back flexing through his shirt.

"Lexi why don't you come and help me in the

kitchen with the cinnamon buns," Mom said, diverting my attention away from Drew.

"All right, Mom." I closed the box I was sifting through and followed her into the kitchen.

I stood at the counter while she pulled apart the buns from the pan and plated them up before drizzling the sticky sugar topping onto them.

"I see you have grandma's angel necklace on. You normally only wear that when you are wishing for something."

I sighed and shrugged my shoulders. "I guess I just felt like being close to her right now."

"Lexi are you sure everything is okay?"

I toyed with telling her about how I was feeling for Drew and was just about to say something when I heard someone behind me.

"Finally got the tree up," Drew said, coming into the kitchen to wash his hands. "It is a great tree, Lexi. You really did pick the perfect one." He turned to face us, smiling at me while he dried his hands.

"Thanks!" I noticed my mother watching me in the questioning way all mothers did. "These ready now, Mom?" I questioned and grabbed three of the plates and scurried into the living room, setting the plates beside the tray of drinks that Mom had brought in earlier.

Mom had more apple cider heating on the stove by the time the cinnamon buns had been eaten. We were all in the living room starting to decorate the tree. The lights had already been put on the tree and were now twinkling away. I pulled the next ornament from the box and unwrapped it from its tissue. I inhaled when I saw the ornament I had in my hand and tears filled my eyes.

I held the ornament in my hands, turning it over and over. Two red rubies formed the head and dress of the angel, secured together by a set of sterling silver wings. "This was grandma's angel. I remember she told me that grandpa gave it to her when he returned home from the war. I remember her always telling me it had such a special meaning behind it, but she never got the chance to tell me what it was."

Mom sat down beside me and took the ornament in her hand. "I haven't seen this in years." She sniffled. "What box did you find it in?"

"This one right here," I said, pointing to it.

"Funny, I'm sure I had that box down last year. I don't remember seeing it," she said, looking it over, a soft smile coming to her lips.

"Do you know what the story or special meaning is behind it is, Mom?" I asked, folding the tissue paper that it had been wrapped in and placing it back in the box.

"I do. You see, grandpa was never supposed to return from the war the Christmas he gave her this. He was supposed to go on another two tours before he was discharged from the Army. He was sent home on a two-day relief just before Christmas and he surprised her with this ornament. He said he always wanted to be with her, even though he was far away, and that this angel would watch over her while he was gone. He was deployed two days later as scheduled, and grandma was beside herself. She was convinced he wasn't going to be coming home to her.

"Anyways, she prayed every night to that angel to send him back to her, and two weeks later, on Christmas Eve, grandpa showed up on the doorstep, surprising her. When she asked him what he was doing back, he explained that two days after he had been deployed, he got a strange feeling in his gut, one that wouldn't leave. Apparently, he requested to be discharged and pulled out of the deployment. Since the deployment was voluntary, they granted him that and sent him home. He got word two days after Christmas that on Christmas day, the troops he had been with had stumbled into a war zone and were caught in gunfire. Every one of the soldiers he had been with were killed."

I wiped the tears that fell from my eyes and looked over to where Zack and Drew sat. Both had tears in their eyes as well.

"This," my mother said, picking up the angel that sat on the chain around my neck, "is an exact replica of this one. Grandpa had it made for grandma the month before he died. It had special instructions to be passed down to the first girl born in the family, which is you, Lexi."

I smiled and held the angel pendant tight in my hand.

"Why don't you put the ornament on the tree, Lexi," Mom sniffled, handing it over to me.

I took the angel from her and walked over to the tree, placing it right near the top. I stood looking at it for a minute, grasping the angel charm around my neck, thinking back to the last Christmas grandma had with us.

I sat in the dimly lit kitchen, everything now cleaned and put away from dinner, staring down into the cup of hot peppermint tea that sat in front of me. Mom and Dad had gone off to a banquet on the other end of town. Zach and Drew had gone to the store for some snack food. I was glad to have this time alone after what Mom and Dad had told us at dinner. It wasn't something that I was expecting, and it had completely thrown me for a loop. They announced that they were getting rid of my childhood home, the only place I knew to come for comfort when I needed it. They wanted to downsize and move somewhere warmer, sunnier, and smaller.

I looked over to the pantry door and saw the familiar black marks on the doorframe that told us how much we had grown over the years. There were even marks there for Drew, because they always wanted to make sure that he felt a part of the family.

I breathed in deeply, trying to figure out what I would do when I no longer had this home to come to, but nothing was coming to mind. A tear slipped down my cheek and I quickly wiped it away when I heard the front door open and close. I stayed where I was, hoping that no one saw me sitting alone in the dark. I really didn't want to be bothered with anyone or anything.

I kept my head down, looking into that steaming cup of tea, when I felt two strong hands grip my shoulders. "What do you say, Lex, want some cake?" Drew asked, walking around the island and pulling out the coconut cream cake from the fridge.

"Please," I whispered.

He cut two rather large pieces, plated them, and slid one in front of me, holding out a fork for me to take. As I reached for it, he pulled it away, a gorgeous smile plastered on his face. I looked up at him but couldn't help the tears in my eyes. The thought of this being our last Christmas in this house was almost too much to bear.

"Lex, what's wrong?"

"Where's Zach?" I asked, trying my best to avoid the inevitable.

"I dropped him off at Ann Marie's." He pulled the chair out beside me and sat down. "So spill it. What's got that pretty head of yours in such a mess?"

I took a forkful of cake and put it in my mouth, trying to figure out how to share with him. "I guess it was the shock of the news that they want to sell the house. I always thought I would spend every Christmas here forever, you know, with my kids. I imagined all of us in that living room drinking apple cider and eating cinnamon buns while decorating the tree, forever."

Drew was quiet and shook his head. "I get it."

"You do?"

"Of course, this is the only home you've known. It's natural for you to feel this way, but honestly, Lex, they are getting older. This place is huge, and I can't even begin to imagine the cost or the work of the upkeep. You aren't here to help, and Zach is in New York. I mean, it's only them, all alone."

"I know, it's just this place holds so many memories."

"I know. It does for me too. You guys were all a big part of my childhood. After all, this is the only real feeling of home and family that I have."

"It just comes as a shock, I guess. I certainly wasn't expecting them to say they were planning on selling." We both took a bite of cake at the same time, chewing in silence. "I wish there was something I could do."

"Lexi, you have to support their decision and understand where they are coming from. I get it, it's not easy. This place holds lots of memories for me too. It holds most of my memories, more than the actual house I grew up in. But memories, Lex, are in your heart and mind, not in some brick and mortar building. I mean, look at tonight, look at what a simple ornament can bring back to your memory."

I felt my lips start to tremble at what Drew had said and began to cry hard now. He was right. It was still hard, but he was right. "Why are you always so sensible?"

"Because your parents practically raised me. If I had stayed with my dad, I am sure I would have ended up where he did: in some alley behind the city mission, holding a brown paper bag." He stood up and wrapped his arms around me, pulling me into him. He kissed the top of my head, squeezing the back of my neck.

"Thanks." I wrapped my arms around his waist and hugged him tightly, inhaling the scent of his cologne.

"What do you say we go for a walk? Get some fresh air? Just relax and forget what they told us tonight."

"That sounds wonderful."

We walked into town and went directly to the little coffee shop in the center of the village. We had barely said a word on the way into town. I wanted her to know I was there for her, but I didn't want to push her. If she didn't want to talk about it, that was okay.

The coffee shop was busy tonight, people who had been out Christmas shopping and skiing and were now coming in to have a warm drink and some food.

"Did you want coffee or hot chocolate?" I asked, pulling out a chair over near the fireplace so Lexi could sit down.

"Coffee." She smiled, pulling off her gloves and rubbing her hands together, warming them.

I removed my hat, coat, and gloves and went over to

the counter and ordered. I soon had two mugs of hot coffee piled high with whipped cream in front of me. "Miss, do you have any of those chocolate shavings you used to put on top?" I asked, glancing over my shoulder to see if Lexi was watching, but she was busy typing away on her phone.

"I do. One second." She went over to the back counter returned carrying a jar. She sprinkled some on top of Lexi's mugs, dark chocolate and white chocolate died red. I thanked the lady and carried the mugs over to the table and set hers in front of her. Her eyes lit up as soon as she saw her mug.

"Oh, my goodness, you remembered," she cried out, laughing.

"Of course." I laughed. I had made the mistake of getting the whipped cream and chocolate shavings on her coffee for her birthday one year and she never had a coffee here without them, except for maybe at home.

I took my coat off and flung it over the back of my chair and sat down, relaxing back, taking a sip of my coffee. Lexi looked around the little shop at the Christmas decorations that were displayed, and a look of sadness came over her face.

"What is it?"

"Nothing. I guess I've just really missed home, and

it took coming back to figure that part out." She shrugged.

I went to say something, but she stood up and grabbed her camera and went to take pictures of the little Christmas village that the shop always displayed across the fireplace mantel. I sat and watched her get every angle just right and she began clicking away, a sense of peace falling over her face as she captured each little house.

An hour later, as snow lightly fell, we continued our walk through the village. Flakes danced in the air, twinkling in the streetlights as they fell to the ground. I walked beside Lexi as she took more pictures of the people in the village and the beautiful lights of the ski hills. Every click of the camera produced another beautiful photo. I was in awe of how one tiny device could produce a smile like the one she wore. She was beautiful in her element, and just when I averted my eyes from her, she turned the camera toward me and began taking my photo as we walked.

"Are you still living in that condo?" she asked, continuing to snap my photo.

"No, I sold that before...well, before everything went down. I have a small two-bedroom home on the outskirts of the city now. It works well for me. It's not like here, though, where you have your space. My neighbors are literally in my backyard."

"What about work? How is that going?"

"It's been a challenge, but it's going well. I pretty much just buried myself in work after everything happened. It was easier that way, and it kept me busy." I heard the shutter of Lexi's camera go off again, and when I turned, she once again had it pointed at me, a soft smile on her lips as she looked at me through the lens.

"It was pretty tough, eh?"

"Yeah, you could say that. You know, it isn't even the fact that she didn't want to be with me that bothers me, and now I just don't care. What bothered me the most was that I couldn't figure out what the hell happened. We were like glue, totally inseparable. I dropped her off the morning of the wedding, she had her dress in hand, and she ran into the church with a smile on her face, all the girls waiting for her, all of them giggling. Sure, I won't lie, I had cold feet, but I don't think I ever really doubted anything. Well, no, maybe I did, but regardless, she was the one who never made it down the aisle. She just wasn't there."

"I don't think it's you. Even when Zach called and told me, I didn't think it was you."

I listened as the shutter of her camera went off

again and looked in her direction. She was still taking pictures of me as we walked slowly down the street.

"You don't?"

"No, I don't. People grow apart, for reasons sometimes none of us understand. In the end when we finally do understand it, it turns out for the better."

She looked up at me with those blue eyes, and I thought I caught a glimmer of something in them. I cleared my throat and continued walking.

"So, since you asked me earlier, it's my turn. Would you ever move back here?" she asked.

"I could see myself moving here, yes, but like you, I would have to have a reason." I looked over at her and the shutter of her camera went off. I reached over and grabbed the camera from her. "Now that you have objectified me, it's my turn," I said, pulling the camera up to my eye and clicking away as she smiled over at me.

As we walked, I took every opportunity to snap shots of her. She sat down in front of a Christmas planter and posed for a picture, which I gladly took.

"Stand up beside the giant bear over there in front of the pub."

She did as I suggested and once again posed for another picture.

We continued walking in silence until her soft voice

echoed through the air. "So what would give you reason to move back here?"

"Oh, Lex, I don't know. It probably wouldn't happen anytime soon. I'd need a job first. What about you?"

She shrugged, looking over at me, a soft smile on her lips. I quickly raised the camera and snapped away again; only this time, when she looked into the lens, I saw the same glimmer I had seen earlier. Only this time it didn't leave, and it was as if she continued to look right through that lens, right into my eyes and into my soul. I lowered the camera slowly and looked at her. It was definitely there; the glimmer of desire filled her eyes as she looked at me.

I swallowed hard, the look she gave me was mesmerizing, and I slowly dropped my arm that was holding the camera. I stepped toward her, expecting her to back away, but she didn't. Instead, her eyes held mine, and I stepped closer into her and felt her hand slip into my free one. I watched as she lightly licked her full lips, leaving them slightly parted.

"I guess if I had someone here, someone special to me, I might move back," she whispered to me, her eyes still burning with desire as she studied mine.

I knew instantly that she wasn't talking about

family, but I didn't say anything. I just kept my eyes locked on her.

"You know, someone who wanted to be with me."

The snow started falling harder and we stood on the quiet sidewalk staring at one another.

"Someone who maybe loved me, and I them." As the words fell from her lips, her eyes dropped away from mine. "I doubt I'll ever find that though," she whispered.

I cupped her cheek and lifted her head so she was looking at me. The look of hurt in her eyes was apparent, and I wondered who the guy was who had hurt her. A spark of a tear flashed at me as the light hit her eyes, and soon all I wanted to do was find out who he was and what he had done.

I let out a breath, and instead of focusing on that, I slowly leaned into her, my lips barely feathering across hers. I expected her to pull away, possibly slap me, but she didn't. Instead, she stepped into me and placed her hands on my chest, and I kissed her again, this time deeper, my tongue brushing through her mouth.

When she pulled away, she looked up at me, a shy smile coming to her lips, a lone tear sliding down her cheek, but again I didn't focus on that. "You'll find him one day, Lex, I promise, and he is going to be the luck-iest man in the world, trust me." I leaned down, kissing her hard, pulling her small body against mine, and instantly I wished it wasn't winter and that we weren't standing here in thick jackets. I wanted to feel her body pressed into mine.

Lexi let out a soft moan as I kissed her deeper, harder, and I felt my cock jump as she wrapped her arms around my neck.

I was at the counter waiting for the two coffees I had ordered, my mind reeling from what I had learned at dinner. They were really selling the house; they had mentioned it earlier through the year, but I never figured it would happen. I let out a breath. I really needed tonight with Ann Marie. I needed the distraction because I would be lying if I said them selling the house wasn't bothering me. I knew it had bothered Lexi. I mean, the tears were practically running down her cheeks before the words had even left my parents' lips. I'm pretty sure on some weird level it bothered Drew as well.

I hadn't called Ann Marie to tell her I was even dropping by; I just had Drew drop me off. I had gone into the house and asked her to join me for a walk into town. After an hour, I still hadn't mentioned anything. I knew she knew something was on my mind, but she was giving me space, just like she always had, and she would listen when I was ready to talk about it.

Two coffees were placed on the counter in front of me. "Enjoy, sir."

I smiled at the girl who had pulled me from my inner thoughts and picked up the two mugs and carried them over to the table.

"Your peppermint latte, my love." I placed the mug in front of Ann Marie and sat down across from her, both of us taking a sip.

"So, I think I decided on the necklace for my mom," she said, setting her cup down and looking at me. "However, I'm still torn. I really liked the heart pendant, but then just the simple chain was nice too, that way she could wear one of her own pendants."

"I like either idea, but perhaps if you are really undecided, we could always go back and look again."

"That might be a good idea. What about you? Did you decide on anything?"

I let out a deep breath. The trouble was what I wanted to do for my parents and what I could do were two very different and far apart things, especially with a wedding approaching. I let out a sigh.

"Zach what is it?" Ann Marie asked, resting her hand on mine. "You seem distracted."

"Mom and Dad are selling the house," I answered, glancing out the window of the cafe, shoppers rushing by carrying their purchases, smiles on their faces. "They told us tonight at dinner."

"Oh, Zach, I'm so sorry." She placed her hand on my forearm. "Lexi must be a mess! I know how much she loves that house. I also know how hard this year has been on her. Did you ask her what she thought?" Ann Marie asked, now giving me all of her attention.

"You would have cried if you could have seen her face when they told us tonight. She's crushed. She has been traveling all over, and as you said, it's been a hard year for her, and she comes home to this news. The tears were practically on her cheeks as the words fell from Mom's lips. I haven't had a chance to talk to her about it though. Drew and I left the house right after dinner, and then I had him drop me off at your place. I needed my own time to digest everything."

"That's understandable, Zach."

"I just wish there was a way for us to keep the house for them, or perhaps help them out throughout the year. I know if they had help, they would stay."

"Well, maybe you should talk to Lexi and see if she

feels the same way, then perhaps you guys could, I don't know, help out on some level."

"I just don't know how. I mean, she lives in Italy, for crying out loud. It's not like she can just hop in her car and come home for a weekend," I said, letting out a laugh. "Which means the lion's share would land on me."

"Is she going back?"

"What do you mean? Of course, she is. She is only home for a couple of weeks. Why?"

"Nothing. It's not my place to say anything, Zach."

"Oh no, what do you know that the rest of us don't?"

"That, my love, is for Lexi to share with everyone." Ann Marie smiled at me and nodded toward the window. "Speak of the devil."

I looked out the window in the direction that Ann Marie had gestured just in time to see Drew and Lexi walk by. Lexi had her camera in her hand taking photos of someone across the street, with Drew walking beside her. "Well, I guess I won't have to wait too long, since they are right over there."

Ann Marie smiled at me. "How about we finish our donut and coffee, and then we can go meet them. It looks like they will be down here for a while anyways."

She placed her hand over mine once again in a comforting gesture.

"That sounds great!" I said, leaning in for a kiss. As we parted, the waitress dropped our two fresh donuts in front of us.

Once we finished, we bundled back up and made our way out into the street. "They couldn't have gone very far," I said, looking both ways before stepping into the street with Ann Marie in tow. She grabbed hold of my gloved hand, following me down one of the side streets. As we turned down the third street on our right, I stopped in my tracks, abruptly enough that Ann Marie ran right into my back.

"Zach, what on earth?"

I couldn't answer her. I was in shock. There in front of me was my little sister—my sweet little sister—locking lips with my best friend.

Ann Marie pulled on the arm of my jacket, signaling to me what I already saw. She leaned in, whispering, "Zach we should go. Leave them be." She pulled on my hand to pull me away from the scene in front of me, but my feet were glued to the ground.

Alexa

It was as if the world had stopped spinning. The only thing I heard was the whooshing of my own pulse in my ears, my heart pounding hard in my chest as I closed my eyes. The feel of Drew's lips on mine, his taste, the way he ran his tongue through my mouth... I didn't want the moment to end. He was an amazing kisser, soft, gentle, yet I could feel the urgency and want behind it. As his tongue swept across mine one more time, I could feel the intensity of the throbbing between my legs and wished we weren't standing in the middle of a street so he could put his hands on me.

Our lips parted, and I looked up into his blue eyes, the world around us coming back into focus. He was looking down at me, nothing being said between us.

We just stood looking at one another for what felt like hours. He leaned in slowly, cupped my cheeks, and kissed me again, his lips gently brushing against mine.

I felt his hands start to move through my jacket, down my back, stopping just above my ass we heard a man clear his throat behind us. Instantly, Drew jumped away from me as if I had bitten him, causing me to jump as well. I was just about to protest when Zach came into focus.

He had been the one to clear his throat, the one who had interrupted our very first kiss. Zach. My brother. I could feel my cheeks heating with embarrassment as Zach's eyes burned into mine, and suddenly I felt like a child caught with something I shouldn't have.

Ann Marie stood there with a small, uncomfortable smile on her face. She said nothing, probably trying to hide her embarrassment for intruding on us. Zach, on the other hand, stood there glaring at me before his eyes turned to Drew.

"Look, Zach, it's not what you think," Drew instantly said, holding his hands up in an innocent gesture, probably afraid Zach was going to hit him.

Ann Marie placed her hand on Zach's chest and whispered something to him.

"Sure, sure. What do you think this looks like?" Zach bit out, the tension between them surrounding us all. The tension was almost too much to take, and suddenly I was afraid that perhaps Drew had been right in trying to defend himself.

I could see the tension in my brother's body, and without thinking, I stepped between them, trying to stop a fight before it even started, but knowing full well that I wouldn't have a chance if it did. "Both of you stop right now. I'm an adult, Zach, in case you've forgotten."

"Never said you weren't."

"Then what is your problem?"

Zach didn't take his eyes from Drew for what felt like an eternity, and then started to shake his head, appearing to let the situation go. "Look, honestly, I don't give a shit about what goes on between the two of you, but I highly suggest that you both think twice about it. It's not a good idea."

I frowned at my brother. I was more than pissed off with him. I was furious. "How dare you say something like that, Zach. Drew, let's go." I turned and grabbed Drew's hand, pulling him with me, but the instant my eyes met Drew's, I knew from the look he gave me that whatever had happened here wouldn't happen again.

"Drew?" I pleaded as he stood there glancing between my brother and me.

"Lexi, I'm sorry, but I just remembered I have something I've got to do." He looked down at me and dropped my hand.

I stood there, not sure what to say, as I watched him back away from us, finally tearing his eyes from mine. As he walked away from me, I fought the tears and the need to run after him. I felt like I was glued to my spot, my feet heavy and my heart hurting.

"Lexi, I'm sorry," I heard Zach say as I glanced over his shoulder to see if I could still see Drew, but he was already gone. Zach cleared his throat, pulling my attention to him. "Lexi, I'm sorry. I came over because I saw you earlier and wanted to talk about Mom and Dad and the situation with the house."

I tore my eyes from the direction Drew had gone off in and glared at my brother. "Look, if they want to move, who are we to stop them," I bit out. I was angry and now worried about Drew.

"I just figured you'd be upset, and that between us, maybe we could figure out a way to help them keep it."

I kept my focus in the direction that Drew had gone off in. "We'll talk at home. I can't do this right now. I have to go."

I ran from where Zach and Ann Marie stood and headed in the direction Drew had gone off in, sure that he was probably already long gone. I walked in a panic up and down the streets, stopping to ask a few people if they had seen someone by his description, but no one could help me. I spent the next forty minutes basically walking the same blocks in desperation to find him, but he was nowhere to be found.

After another forty minutes, I finally stopped. I was cold and exhausted. I was back at the coffee shop and decided to go inside to see if Drew was there.

I wandered in and took a seat by the fireplace, removing my jacket and letting the heat sink into me. I pulled my phone from my pocket, quickly checking my text messages, praying that he had messaged me, but there was nothing from him, only from my brother. Defeated, I let out a breath, quickly sent a text, and then headed to the counter to order a coffee.

The only sound I heard was the crunching of the snow under my boots as I slowly walked up the hill back to the house. It had gotten colder in the hours that I'd been gone, and snow was falling harder now. I zipped my jacket up and wrapped my scarf up around my ears before placing my hood over my head. I shoved my gloved hands into my pockets, trying to warm them.

I was glad when the house came into view. The windows were all dark, Lexi probably having gone to bed long ago. The driveway was now empty. Zach must have come and picked up the car and was still with Ann Marie, and Barb and Jim had gone over to a charity banquet and were spending the night there.

I made my way quietly up the front steps and sat down on the rocking chair that always sat outside the front door, regardless of the season. I glanced at my watch. It was close to midnight; I should have been in bed hours ago, not out wandering the streets. I let out a deep sigh, listening to the silence around me and thinking about how good a hot shower and coffee would be right about now as a shiver ran through me.

I had walked around town for the last three and a half hours thinking about tonight and the situation that Zach had found Lexi and me in. I thought long and hard about what I was going to do. I knew I had made the right decision and that was to move on and pretend that nothing had ever happened between us, but that already felt wrong. As soon as I had resigned myself to that decision, the memories came back and I thought back to tonight.

Watching Lexi had been amazing, and so was spending time with her. There was something so light and refreshing about her presence that it calmed the endless ache in me. Spending time with her also completely ended the thoughts of Laura, something that hadn't happened in the last six months, no matter how hard I had tried to shut it off.

I thought back to the moment when I had realized I

was going to kiss her, how calm and relaxed I had felt. It was our first kiss. Surely there should have been nervousness with it, but there was nothing. Instead, everything just ebbed and flowed in perfect harmony. She had felt perfect in my arms, and as my lips danced across hers, I felt my soul ignite with something I had never ever felt before.

That all ended when I had heard Zach clear his throat. That fire had died and was replaced with a feeling that I had been caught doing something that I shouldn't. Even though I knew we were both adults, I could tell by the look in his eyes that it bothered him to see me with his sister. Zach had been my best friend for years. The whole family had welcomed me with loving arms, and the last thing I wanted was not to be wanted. They were all the family I had.

I leaned back in the rocking chair, rubbing my legs with my gloved hands, trying to get some feeling back into them. This was going to be the hardest two weeks of my life. Staying in this house with Lexi right across the hall from my bedroom, practically within arm's reach. There was no way I could do it, I decided.

I pulled my phone from my pocket and looked up local hotels. There had to be somewhere that I could stay. The longer I thought about it, I knew there was absolutely no way I would be able to stay here and not kiss her again. I wouldn't be able to look at her every morning and evening across the dinner table and hide what I was thinking every single second. Plus, if I ran into her in the kitchen again or crossed paths as she left the bathroom like I had done the other day, I would be in big trouble.

I pulled my hood tighter around my head and scrolled through the first website I came to and punched in the respective dates I was looking for and hit search. No vacancy flashed on the screen. By the time I got to the tenth hotel's website, they already had the words "no vacancy" clearly printed right on the front page, saving me the time. It was as if the universe was trying to tell me something. I decided to stop looking within town and began looking up hotels on the outskirts, but again there was nothing.

I pocketed my almost-dead phone and stood to unlock the door and go inside when something caught my eye. A light from the upstairs front window illuminated the snow on the front yard. Lexi was still awake, no doubt waiting to hear from me. She had texted me earlier, and like the scum I was, I'd just ignored her message. There was no way I could go inside now; I didn't want to be confronted by her.

I let out a breath and pulled my glove from my pocket, sliding my hand back into it. Then I tucked my hands into my pockets and sat back down, trying to ignore the fact that I was freezing. Watching the flakes dance down to the ground, I redirected my thoughts away from everything, and that was when I felt my cell phone vibrate in my pocket.

I let out a breath, grabbing it front my pocket, and looked down at the screen. Lexi had sent me another message. I was going to ignore it and open it later, but my phone vibrated again.

Lexi: I hope you are okay.

Lexi: I'm going to bed, but please when you get home just knock on my door.

I closed my eyes and clenched my teeth. She was killing me inside. Finally, the light went off in the upstairs window, leaving the front yard in darkness again. I gave it another ten minutes, until I could no longer stand the fact that my feet were now thoroughly freezing.

I got up and quietly put my key into the lock of the front door. A blast of warm air hit me as soon as I stepped inside, my skin hurting from the abrupt change in temperature. I quietly slid my coat off and hung it up in the closet and removed my wet boots. I ignored the want for a hot coffee and tiptoed upstairs, careful not to make too much noise that would alert her that I was home. I slipped into my room and gathered my sleep pants and one of the towels Lexi had left for me last night and quickly and quietly made my way to the shower.

I stared up at my bedroom ceiling, my one hand flung behind my head and the other resting on my tummy, trying hard to relax. I had sent Drew a text over half an hour ago and he still hadn't responded. I was worried. There was no reason why he shouldn't be talking to me. I thought back to tonight and how wonderful it had been, until Zach happened and drove Drew away. I had dreamed of kissing Drew and so much more since the night he had told me I was beautiful, which was so silly. I mean, that had been ages ago. He probably didn't even remember that night. However, to me, it had made such a difference.

It was the night of my junior prom, and even though he was probably only being nice, his words had meant the world. I let out a breath and thought back to that night. I could remember it like it was yesterday.

I walked down the stairs dressed in the white and pink prom dress that I had so loved up until Rickie Hansen had canceled on me and left me in a fit of tears for three straight days right before my junior prom. I hadn't wanted to go anymore. In fact, I had begged my mother to take the dress she had bought back and to leave me to wallow in my room. She wouldn't hear of it and had instead she taken me to get my hair and nails done in preparation for tonight.

As I left the safety of my room, looking like a large bath puff, I made my way downstairs to wait for my ride. I could hear Zach and Drew in the living room playing video games and couldn't wait for the jokes to start.

As my bare foot hit the landing, both Drew and Zach turned their eyes from the TV and onto me. I awkwardly smiled. I hated everything about this dress now and felt completely stupid going to junior prom all alone.

"You look nice, sis," Zach said, getting up to get more snacks and drinks from the kitchen.

"Sure, Mom probably made you say that," I called after him.

As soon as he was out of sight, Drew stood up from where he had been sitting and came over to me.

"You ready for tonight?" he asked, shoving his hands deep into his jeans pockets and shrugging his shoulders.

"I guess. I don't really even know why I'm bothering to go, to be honest. All my friends have dates. I'm just going to be the annoying third wheel."

Drew looked down at me and smiled. "I know how you feel. I went to my junior prom alone. Don't tell your brother; he thinks I went with a date," he whispered, and I let out a tiny laugh.

"No worries, your secret is safe with me," I said, placing my hand over my heart.

"So, did your brother give you his lecture yet? He's been practicing it on me for the last month." He grinned.

"What lecture?" I asked, rolling my eyes and giving him a questioning look.

"To stay away from the bad ones?"

"The bad ones?"

"Yeah, you know, the bad guys, the ones who are only after one thing." He waggled his eyebrows, gesturing to what he meant.

I felt my cheeks redden at his suggestion. "He hasn't said anything."

"All right, well, I feel it then my duty as your brother's best friend to do it on his behalf. Don't let them near you, Lexi. I'm sure they will be buzzing around you like bees to honey." His eyes dropped down my body, causing me to blush again.

When he noticed that I had become a little uncomfort-

able, he smiled. Zach came in the room carrying a bowl of popcorn and two small bottles of coke. Drew instantly grabbed my hand and twirled me around, letting out a low whistle as I spun around for him. "You look amazing, Lexi, really. Have a great time, eh?" he said in an attempt to change the subject.

"Stop hitting on my sister, dude. It's bloody disgusting."

"I'm not," Drew protested.

Zach flopped back down on the couch, grabbing the gaming controller, un-pausing the game, and killing off Drew's character. Drew looked at me, winked, and turned around and went and joined Zach. Both became engrossed in their game and ignored me.

I'd remembered not knowing what to say to his pep talk of sorts, but I still remembered how he had looked at me as I stood in front of him that night. The way his eyes had washed over my body was the same way his eyes followed me out the front door, and the exact same way he had looked at me the other night in the kitchen.

I rolled over in bed and looked at the clock. I was getting worried. It was cold out and the snow had been falling hard for the last hour. I let out a breath, and then I heard the hallway floor creak and the sound of a door opening and closing. It had to be Drew. Mom and Dad were staying overnight at the hotel the banquet was being held at, and Zach had long ago messaged me, first to apologize, and then to let me know he was spending the night at Ann Marie's.

I got up off my bed and opened my bedroom door, glancing out through the crack. Drew's bedroom door was open, a soft light spilling out into the hallway. I watched for a minute through the crack of my door, then I saw Drew. He came walking out of his bedroom, shirtless, his jeans undone and hanging sexily on his waist. His towel was flung over his shoulder, and he carried his toiletry bag in his other hand. He ran his hand through his hair, turning it into a rather disheveled, sexy-looking mess, which was hot as hell. I was about to call out to him but thought twice, mainly because I didn't really know what to say. He went into the bathroom, shutting the door, but still left it open a crack.

I quickly shut my door and rested my back against the cool panel. I wanted more of what I had tonight, and it wasn't fair to me that Zach had interrupted us. I wanted to be held in Drew's arms. I wanted the smell of his skin invading every part of me. I wanted to feel his large, strong hands gripping parts of my body that they shouldn't.

I opened the door to my bedroom a crack and peeked out into the hallway. Drew padded back across the hall to his room and came back out carrying his sleep pants in his hand, and back into the bathroom he went once again, leaving the door open a crack. I heard the shower turn on.

I turned back against my wall, inhaled deeply trying to calm my heavily beating heart, and tiptoed out of my room and over to the bathroom door. I peeked through the crack, careful not to be seen. He stood with his back to the door, dropping his jeans. They pooled around his feet, his belt buckle clinking hard on the tile floor.

I turned my head from the crack in the bathroom door and bit my lip. My heart was beating so hard I felt like I might faint. I stood there for a second, trying to catch my breath, and then turned back to take another peek. The only glimpse I caught was his muscular bare leg as he climbed into the frosted shower and shut the door.

I made my way back to my bedroom, shutting the door quietly behind me. A funny feeling crept into the pit of my stomach as an idea popped into my mind. Sure, I was under my parents' roof, but they weren't here right now. It was only Drew and me. No one would have to know anything happened between us, but us.

"No, you are not going to do it, Lexi. You are going to get back into bed," I said under my breath to the empty room and crawled back under my warm covers. I laid there staring up at the ceiling, listening to the water run. Minutes later, I climbed back out of bed. I pulled my shirt over my head, letting it fall to the floor, the cold air of the room causing my nipples to harden right away. I let out a breath and dropped my pants to the floor. I walked over to my full-length mirror and looked at my naked body, my mind running rampant with questions: Would he be attracted to me? Would he push me away and send me back to my room? Was I taking a huge chance on ruining our friendship by doing this? I ran my hands over the flat of my belly, took a deep breath, and with shaking hands, opened my bedroom door and went to claim what I wanted.

Drew

I closed my eyes as the hot water showered down on me. The heat felt good on my cold, aching body. I had spent too much time out in that cold due to my stubbornness of not wanting to run into her again tonight once I returned. I deserved to be cold. I was trying hard to let thoughts of Lexi wash away, but no matter how hard I had tried to get her and that kiss out of my mind, it seemed to come back twice as powerful than before.

I thought back to the simple things: the way she blinked up at me as she opened her eyes after I had first kissed her; the look she gave to me as I looked at her through the camera lens; her sexy eyes full of lust and desire as she had stared back at me. Just the simple thought of that look caused my already hard cock to start throbbing. I thought back to the other night as she reached up to grab the glass out of the cupboard and how her T-shirt had ridden up to show me her ass in those black panties. Her perfect, round ass peeking out at me, ripe like a peach that I just wanted to sink my teeth into.

I reached down, taking my thick cock in my hand, squeezing the shaft and almost moaning out loud at how good it felt. I placed one hand against the shower wall, tilted my head back, and closed my eyes as I started to rub the length of my cock. It was nothing but me, the sound of the water hitting the floor of the shower...and the sound of the shower door opening behind me.

Biting my bottom lip, I opened my eyes and blinked hard. Lexi stood there, naked in front of me, like a dream. I blinked hard again and watched as she stepped into the shower and closed the door behind her. Her cheeks flushed as my eyes traveled the length of her body. I noticed her gaze was firmly planted on my hand, which was gripping my cock. She bit her bottom lip as she locked eyes with me for a second before she looked back down at my hand. Shy little Lexi, who wasn't so shy anymore, stared at the full length of my cock in my hand.

Neither of us said anything as she stepped closer to

me and ran her hands down my chest and over my abs, taking my cock in her hand, the trail of her touch burning my skin. She stroked me, squeezing my thick, hard cock, looking me directly in the eye. Her cheeks were flushed, and she bit her bottom lip as she looked up innocently at me. Only there was nothing innocent about Lexi now, and I watched as the water ran down over her breasts, the stream dripping from her nipples.

The rational part of my brain finally kicked in what seemed like minutes later. I shouldn't be here with her like this. This couldn't happen; it would ruin everything. I reached down and took her hand in mine, and as hard as it was, I removed her hand from my hard, aching cock before this went any further.

"Lexi, we shouldn't do this." That was all I could get out, the look in her eyes eating me alive as she pulled her hand from mine and began working her hands over me again. I had to let go of hers to hold onto the walls of the shower as she stroked me. She was killing me. "Lex, this is going to change everything," I murmured as she placed her lips against mine.

"Good," she whispered before she lowered herself to her knees.

I looked down at her, as she looked up at me, and I watched as she licked the head of my cock. One single lick that sent a wave of heat through my body so intense I felt like I could combust. I let my head drop back and I held back the moan I so badly wanted to let out. I didn't want to encourage her, but that didn't work. She could already tell from my response that I had loved it.

She trailed her tongue from the base of my shaft all the way to the tip, swirling her tongue around the head. When I opened my eyes and looked down at her, all I saw was her lust-filled, heavy eyes staring back at me. I was in trouble. She knew I was watching her, she knew I liked what I saw, and this time she wrapped her lips around my cock and I watched it disappear into her mouth, all while she continued looking up at me.

I wrapped my hand in her thick brown mane and squeezed. Her mouth felt fucking amazing. I closed my eyes and inhaled a sharp breath as she continued to slowly devour my cock, even paying attention to my balls, cupping them in her soft hand.

I kept a grip on her hair, resting my hand on the back of her head as I let my head drop back and just enjoy everything that she was doing to me. I felt her other hand rest on my hips as she continued to suck my cock. This time as she took me deep in her mouth, the tip of my cock hitting the back of her throat, and I couldn't help but let a throaty groan escape. I could already feel myself starting to swell. She didn't seem to mind, and she took me even deeper, so deep that I could feel the head of my cock hitting the back of her throat.

Three more times of the intense feeling of almost slipping down her throat and I couldn't hold back any longer. My orgasm ripped out of me, and I held her head as I shot hot cum down her throat. I could feel her throat reflexes swallowing every single drop of me.

I eased off my grip on the back of her head and felt myself slide out of her hot mouth. I opened my eyes. She was still on her knees before me, looking up at me with a knowing look in her eyes. I took both of her hands and pulled her up and into me, kissing her lips.

I could barely wait to touch her, to feel the weight of her breasts in my hands and bury myself deep inside of her. I pushed her against the wall, turning her so her back was to me. I pulled her against my body, kissing the side of her neck, my hands gripping her breasts, my thumbs running over her nipples. My right hand trailed down the flat of her stomach, between her legs, my fingers running between her slick folds, and she let out a tiny moan. She was already wet, and I continued running my finger over her clit while I bit and sucked on her neck. Her head fell back onto my shoulder, her arms coming up behind her head as she let out a deep, sexy moan, her lips meeting mine.

I turned her back around, pushing her back up against the shower wall, and bent down, taking a nipple into my mouth. I ran my tongue back and forth over her nipple and gently bit and teased her, my hand quickly finding its way between her legs again, inserting two fingers inside of her as my thumb rubbed her clit. I wrapped my arm around her waist, supporting her when I felt her start to shake. She was so close to coming I could practically taste it. I dropped to my knees, taking her leg and resting it on my shoulder, and looked up at her. "You ready?" I asked.

She shyly nodded her head, her cheeks and chest flushed pink, her breathing rapid. I spread her lips with my fingers and ran my tongue back and forth over her clit. I couldn't get enough of the taste of her. She ran her hands through my hair, fisting a handful as I kept running my tongue over the swollen bundle of nerves, her moans getting louder.

"Drew...." She fisted my hair tighter. I didn't stop. I just continued until she exploded in my mouth, screaming my name.

Completely out of breath, I leaned against the shower wall, my legs shaking, trying my hardest to regain my composure. I felt Drew slip his arms around my waist and pull me under the water. He kissed me deeply before turning the water off. He opened the shower stall and grabbed one of the towels, passing it to me. I quickly dried my hair and wrapped the towel around my body. I watched as he wrapped one of the towels around his waist, and then stepped toward me. He softly smiled, and then placed one hand on each side of my head and leaned in for yet another kiss. His lips danced over mine, his tongue sweeping through my mouth. Looking down into my eyes, we just stood there looking at one another, saying things between the two of us silently.

He stepped out of the shower and reached for my hand, guiding me out of the bathroom, into the hall, and across to my room. I thought he was going to kiss me good night and run off to his room, but he surprised me by following me inside and kicking my door closed.

I stood at the edge of my bed, holding my towel against me. Drew turned, studying me. The look in his eyes was one I had only seen a few short minutes ago before he went down on me, devouring me. He took a sure step toward me, dropping his towel to the floor, and my eyes instantly traveled to his already hardened cock.

"Like what you see?" he asked, his words brushing over me and causing me to shiver.

I slowly nodded my head as he stepped closer and pulled my hands away from my chest where I was holding the towel tightly around me. As soon as my hands were in his, my towel slipped down my body and fell into a heap on the floor. His eyes never left mine as his hands gently held mine.

"You're sure this is what you want?" he murmured as his eyes trailed over my body.

I nodded, suddenly feeling very shy and exposed. "Yes." I swallowed hard.

"You're absolutely certain?" he said, his lips brushing lightly against mine.

I knew we were about to cross that imaginary line where friendship would no longer exist if we didn't work out. Instead of that scaring me like it should have, a weird comfort came over me. I didn't reply. Instead, I reached down between us and ran my hand over his hard cock and watched as he closed his eyes and dropped his head back.

"I'm sure. I want you, Drew," I whispered.

I sat down on the edge of my bed, scooting over so he too could climb in. He placed his arm under my head and threw the blankets over us. He kissed me deeply while his free hand cupped my breast, his thumb running over my nipple. I fought to keep the moan from escaping my mouth and gripped his cock, running my thumb through the bead of precum that was sitting there.

"Do you have a condom?" he asked between kisses.

I shook my head no, feeling almost as if this was the way for fate to step in and end us before we started.

"Don't go anywhere. I'll be right back," he whispered, kissing me again. He grabbed the towel from the floor and darted out my door, and within seconds he was back holding two condoms between his teeth.

"Get on your knees," he murmured, dropping the towel as I heard the telltale sign of the package ripping.

I did as he asked and looked over my shoulder to

see him finish rolling the condom on. The other guys I had been with in the past had been passive. I wanted one to take control. I wanted *him* to take control. I'd had control over every area of my life, and for one once I didn't want to think about how the night should go.

I spread my legs and kneeled at the edge of the bed and bent down so my forearms were supporting me. When I could feel the heat from his body behind me, I closed my eyes. I felt powerless as his large, strong hands gripped my waist, pulling me back against him.

"Feel that?" he murmured. "Feel how hard I am for you?"

His words sent a chill through me, hardening my nipples, and instantly I let out a moan. I was expecting to feel the pressure of him at my opening, but instead I felt his fingers slide through my wetness from my clit to my opening. When he did it again, a light moan escaped my mouth, begging him to do it again. He didn't give in. Instead, his hand ran over my ass, lightly spanking me.

"Ready for me?" his thick voice asked.

"Yes." I swallowed hard, finally feeling the pressure of him at my opening. I took a deep breath as he began inching into me. He took his time, sliding in just a bit, and then out again, letting me adjust to him until my body was practically begging for him. I was dripping by the time he was fully seated inside of me, filling me, stretching me. Then I felt him pull back, leaving me empty and wanting for only a second when he pushed back into me, satisfying the empty space. He held my hips tightly as he continued this rhythm, slow, deep, and steady. It didn't take long for me to start tightening around him, but instead of letting me come, he pulled out and guided me to my back. I lay there looking up at him, begging him with my eyes to sink deeply into me.

"Lexi." His voice was tight, almost as if he were unsure he should continue. I grabbed his hands and sat up to meet his lips, pulling him down to me. He kneeled on the edge of the bed and slid back into me. His pace was slower, gentler as his lips met mine. The slower he went, the more powerful I could feel my orgasm building. I gripped at his back, digging my nails into him as my orgasm ripped through me. He thrust deeply inside of me one more time, and a deep groan escaped from his lips and his muscles tensed as he emptied himself inside of me moaning my name in my ear.

I rested my head on Drew's shoulder, my eyes closed, my right leg wrapped around his body, and inhaled his manly scent. He held me tightly against him, running his fingers lightly over my arm.

"Tell me what it was like?" I whispered. Since I had laid eyes on Drew, I had noticed he wasn't the same man I had known all those years. The spark in his eyes was gone and was replaced with an emptiness I didn't like seeing.

"What was what like?"

"What was it like, her not showing up and leaving you there?"

Drew blew out a breath and adjusted so he was lying on his side. "It was a bit humiliating at first, standing in front of five hundred people, but then this feeling of calm came over me, and suddenly I felt happy. Happy that she had decided not to walk down that aisle. I can't explain it, but all that morning I had been fighting a feeling I couldn't grasp. Everyone thought it was just cold feet." He exhaled and kissed my forehead. "I guess for me the worst part wasn't the fact that she didn't show up; I was more upset at the fact that everything still needed to be paid for. Which sounds so awful."

I let out a tiny laugh at his answer. "So, you weren't as upset as Zach let on?"

"No, and what makes me angry now is that people are still coddling me as if I am some sort of broken human being, but honestly, Lex, that is my answer. I'm not all that upset."

"Really?"

"Yes, and you know you are the only person who has ever asked what really happened from my point of view. All they keep doing is imposing their feelings on me. What about you? How are you doing now after the news tonight?"

I buried my face into his chest and lay there thinking about the news our parents had dropped on us. "If I tell you something, promise to keep it between us?"

"Of course."

"It's killing me," I whispered. "Mom kept wondering why I came home and brought all my stuff. I'm lonely, Drew. People think I have the coolest job in the world, getting to travel and see all these amazing places. It's the exact opposite. I miss everything. I miss birthdays, and holidays, and time just spent with my family."

"Do you think it would help if you came home more often?"

"Well, it might have, but really, I don't have a choice now."

"What do you mean?"

"I don't want to do it anymore. I had planned to come home, get a job here, and surprise them with the news that I was moving back here. Only now, I don't have a choice."

"Why is that?"

"Earlier this year, I got involved with my boss. I know, stupid, right? I had always vowed I wouldn't do it, but I did. Things weren't working out between us, and so he fired me. I've done some work here and there, but I have nothing permanent. So I gave up my apartment before I came home. Now not only do I have no place or job to move back to, but they are selling this place." My eyes blurred over with tears. "I'm a failure."

"Hey, hey, Lex, shhhh. You aren't a failure. It'll be okay," he said, pulling me into him. He held me tightly, not saying anything more.

"I'm sorry," I said, pulling out of his embrace and reaching for a tissue. "This isn't the right time or place to start this." I dabbed at my eyes, wiping away the tears, and pulled away from Drew's embrace.

"It's the perfect time for this. It's okay, really. You don't have to be sorry. You can be real with me; I mean we just... What else has got you worried?"

"The thought of failing. What if after Christmas I can't find a job and decide to go back, get a job there, and fail again?"

He sat up, wrapping his arms around me and pulling me back down with him. "You listen to me. I know you, Lexi. Most people would crumble at the thought of leaving home and living halfway around the world alone. I have always admired you. No matter what life presents to you, you take it and make the best of it, and even if you are struggling, you fight hard and end up landing on your own two feet."

I felt a tear roll down my cheek at his words as he looked into my eyes. He cupped my cheek with his hand, his thumb wiping away the tear, and kissed me deeply.

"You are going to be fine. You always are," he whispered into my mouth, kissing me again.

This moment right here explained to me the exact reason why I had very little ties to any other men. My heart beat gently in my chest, when normally it would have been beating wildly with anticipation of what was to come, and it answered a lot of questions in that moment. Somewhere deep inside of me, I knew who the person was that belonged to me. In a blink of an eye, a calm came over me that I had never experienced before. His kiss took away all the anxiety and panic I had been feeling only seconds before.

I heard the crinkle of the condom wrapper as he reached for it, and I welcomed him with open arms when he slid inside of me and began to make love to me for the second time tonight. As we orgasmed together, my soul spoke to me, screaming loudly. It was him. I had been traveling the world looking for him, and he had been right in my backyard the entire time.

Drew

I blinked hard as the early-morning light started to creep through the slats of the blinds in Lexi's room. I rubbed my eyes and looked over at the clock that sat on her nightstand. It was almost six, and I feared her parents would probably be home soon. As much as I didn't want to, I slid my arm out from underneath Lexi's neck and unwrapped my body from hers, careful not to wake her. She stirred but quickly fell back into her deep sleep. She was exhausted; we'd stayed up talking and had another round between the sheets before we both fell asleep around four.

I crept to the door and turned the knob, stepping out into the hallway, turning back once again to look back at the sleeping angel. My cock was already starting to rise at the thought of crawling back into bed with her and sliding myself between those soft, creamy thighs.

I gripped the doorknob tight and pulled her door closed. There was no way I could crawl back into bed with her. All it would take would be for Zach to come home and come in search of her or me and find us in bed together. He would kill me, I already knew it.

Now, if her parents found out that would be a completely different matter. I'd had sex in their house, under their roof, which meant I had totally disrespected the only two people who had taken me in when I'd had nowhere else to go. I'd not only had sex in their house, but with their daughter. But fuck, I wanted her. I wanted her bad.

I trudged across the hall to my bedroom and crawled back into bed, staring up at the ceiling and thinking about my sleeping angel across the hall.

I slept for a couple more hours and at eight I finally dragged myself up and got dressed. I made my way downstairs, passing by Barbara and Jim on my way to the front door. They were both sitting in the front room by the tree, sipping coffee and reading the morning paper.

"Morning, Drew," Jim said, coming up and smacking me on the back. "Would you be able to give me a hand with the outdoor Christmas lights tomorrow? Zach said he would, but he's got to attend a work meeting, and then something with Ann Marie."

"Morning, sir. Sure thing. I'll be down bright and early to give you a hand."

"No breakfast this morning, Drew?" Barbara asked as she picked up the morning paper to discard in the recycling bin.

"I was up early and have already eaten. I have a few errands I have to run today." I grabbed my boots from the corner and slipped them onto my feet. "Is Lexi up yet?" I questioned, matter of fact.

"Haven't seen her yet this morning," Barbara answered.

"Did you need the car? Zach still hasn't returned yet." Jim reached into his pocket and pulled out his keys holding them out in front of me.

"No, sir, I'll be fine. I don't have much to get, and the walk will do me good," I said, running my hand over my stomach.

Jim let out a large belly laugh. "Son, if I had your body, I would give mine away. All right, enjoy yourself," he said, slapping me on the shoulder and heading into the kitchen where Barbara was getting ready to do more of her baking.

I grabbed my coat, hat, and gloves from the closet and stepped outside quickly as I heard Lexi's bedroom door open upstairs. I quickly hopped down the front steps and made my way into town.

As I walked in the cold morning air, quietness surrounding me, I thought about why I had really come on this trip. It wasn't to see everyone in the family and spend time with them; it was to find an answer about my failed almost marriage. It was to try and understand what the hell had happened and how I was going to move on. It was to understand what the hell I had done wrong in that relationship, so I didn't repeat it going forward. It certainly wasn't to bed my best friend's sister and open my heart and mind to a whole new book of problems. However, that was exactly what had happened. My heart ached, and I was already craving to spend time with Lexi. Even now, only a few short hours after I left her, I wanted to be back with her. This was new to me because I had never once felt that way with Laura, and honestly, it scared me.

Just as I came into the town square, I stopped at the coffee shop that Lexi and I had visited last night. *Great, just another reminder*, I thought to myself as I stepped through the doors, the smell of fresh cinnamon rolls in the air. I grabbed a coffee and muffin for breakfast, quickly ate, and made my way to my next stop: the ski shop. It was such a beautiful day, I purchased a lift ticket, new ski pants, and rented some equipment and headed toward the lift.

I had spent the day hitting the slopes; the conditions couldn't have been better. I had lunch alone with my thoughts, and then I hit the slopes again. There was something so freeing about skiing down a hill, wind in your face, mind completely blank from everything.

It was almost seven, and I slowly walked up the hill toward the house. Barbara probably had dinner on the table and was surely waiting for me. However, part of me wasn't in a hurry. I had left my cell phone at the house, somewhat on purpose. I didn't want to be found. I wanted to be alone with my thoughts.

I glanced down at my watch again, this time picking up the pace, starting to feel bad about being gone for so long and making everyone wait for dinner because I wasn't there. Finally, I hit the driveway ten minutes later. It was full of vehicles, telling me that Zach and Ann Marie were probably here as well. I walked up the driveway and glanced up at the front window to see Lexi standing there staring down at me. I noticed a soft smile come to her lips as she waved at me. I inhaled deeply, trying to figure out how I was going to be around her, and stepped through the front door.

"There you are. We were getting ready to call the police," she whispered, giggling, sneaking in to give me a quick kiss on the cheek.

I glanced up at the dining room, praying that no one noticed what had just happened. When I saw that no one had as much as turned around to see who had walked through the front door, I let out the breath I had been holding.

"Hey. I was at the ski resort," I said, bending to untie my boots, not giving in to a returned kiss. "Sorry I'm late, Barbara," I called out, hanging my coat in the hall closet and following Lexi into the dining area where the entire family sat waiting.

"It's okay, Drew. Take a seat by Lexi there," Barbara said, nodding to the only empty seat at the table.

All through dinner, I was quiet, listening to Ann Marie and Zach talk about their plans for tomorrow. I was hoping that Zach and I would be able to hit the slopes tomorrow afternoon after I helped Joe in the morning, but that didn't look like it would be possible. I would need to find something else to keep me occupied then. As that thought crossed my mind, I looked over and saw Lexi watching me, a slight frown on her face.

I looked down at my plate, avoiding eye contact with her. Throughout the day, I had realized what it was that was bothering me so much. It wasn't really what had happened between Lexi and me. After all, we were both grown, consenting adults. It was more the thought of disappointing her that I was afraid of. I couldn't give Laura what she had apparently needed, that much I knew, and I didn't want to do the same to Lexi. It wasn't the fact that my relationship with Zach would be ruined either. That really didn't matter to me because I knew in time that would heal. All that mattered was I cared for Lexi and I didn't want to hurt her. I guess I had more feelings for her than I had realized, and I needed to tread carefully.

After dinner, Lexi cornered me, wanting to go for a walk and spend time together. Instead of doing what my heart wanted, I made the excuse that I needed to get out and call a client. I borrowed the car Zach and I had rented and went for a drive to clear my head. It was a shitty thing to do, lying to her, especially when I saw the look of disappointment on her face as I left the house alone. I felt like a total ass as I walked down the stairs and got into the car because I could feel Lexi watching me through the front room window.

When I finally returned, the house was dark, and I quietly let myself in. I grabbed a bottle of water from the fridge and climbed up the stairs to my room. I was just about to close my bedroom door behind me when I heard a soft voice call my name. I turned and saw Lexi, her door ajar, as she stood against the doorframe in only a T-shirt and panties, her soft, thick brown hair resting on her shoulder.

Even though my brain told me not to, I sauntered over to her door and leaned against the frame. "Yes?" I asked, looking down into her soft, sad eyes.

"I just wanted to say good night," she said, tracing the letters on my shirt. "Is everything okay?" she asked, resting her hands on my chest.

I simply nodded because the words wouldn't come to my lips. I wasn't sure myself if everything was okay between us now. I wasn't sure of anything anymore.

"I'll leave my door open a crack, in case you want to slip over later tonight," she whispered, leaning in and dragging her soft, full lips over mine, the contact instantly going to my cock.

I closed my eyes and felt the softness of her lips, my free hand instantly cupping the cheek of her ass. I pulled her tighter to me, letting her feel how hard I had become in only those two quick seconds she had been in front of me. A creak on the stairs, however, forced me to let her go.

"Go to bed, Lexi," I whispered, and turned to make my way back to my bedroom. I closed the door behind me, leaned against my door, and closed my eyes, letting out the breath I was holding. This girl was going to be death of me this Christmas.

Drew

"Okay, Drew, so the plan is lights up along the edge of the roof, lining all upper windows, and then again the roof of the front porch, again windows, and finally the garage, including the doors," Jim said as he stood over top of the boxes of lights. "Drew, you will have to take the high ground. My knees and hips can't take a ladder anymore."

"Not a problem," I answered and went into the garage. I pulled the extension ladder down from where it hung on the wall, carried it out of the garage, and set it up against the house.

We quietly and quickly unraveled the strands of lights, Jim sorting them into the correct piles for windows and the roof. We plugged each strand in, replacing any broken or nonworking bulbs before putting them up. I took the strand for the garage roof and climbed the ladder quickly, hooking the cords into the hooks that Zach and I had put in a few years back to make this a faster and easier job. Once the garage was done, I quickly took the roofline strands for the house and front porch, climbed the ladder, and secured those lights as well.

"Boys, I have some hot chocolate for you," I heard Barbara call as I climbed back down the ladder to get more lights.

I walked over and took the mug from her, sipping on the hot liquid. It was cold this morning, and I was thankful for the warm drink.

"Did you want the green or red around the upper windows?" I asked, sifting through the strands.

"How about green on Lexi's window, red on ours, and then green on the other," Barbara said.

"Sure thing."

"I'll do the opposite down here on the two living room windows and around the garage doors while you finish the rest," Jim said, coming for a drink as well.

I drank down the rest of my hot chocolate and grabbed the three strands of lights I would need to complete the upper windows. I started at Lexi's room. I just needed to get this wrapped around the casing and be done.

As I began, one of the hooks fell out after rusting off. I grabbed a new one from my pocket and began screwing it in when movement from inside caught my eye. Lexi's bedroom door flung open and she came wandering into her bedroom wrapped in a towel. I slowly continued replacing the screw, trying hard not to peep in on her.

"Please just leave the room," I whispered to myself, but she didn't. Instead, she dropped her towel to the floor, exposing herself to me without knowing it. I hung the first light up slowly on the hook as I patiently watched. "Just get dressed," I whispered. She didn't. Instead, she walked over and laid down on her bed. She laid on her back, her right hand resting on her stomach, gently running her fingers over her soft skin. Skin I longed to touch again. Her left hand came down and rubbed over her breast, her fingers gently rolling the nipple. I felt my cock start to stiffen as I hooked yet another part of the lights up. I closed my eyes. There was no way this could be happening. There was no way I was out here on the roof watching her touch herself. I closed my eyes tightly, saying a silent prayer to the man upstairs as I felt a bead of sweat roll down my back. When I opened them, she was still there, still rolling her nipple between her fingers. I tried to ignore what was happening through that window and quickly began fastening all the lights around the casing. I was just about to step away when I saw her slip her right hand between her legs, her head tilting back as she slowly rubbed herself.

My heart rate accelerated as I continued to watch. I was so hard I was sure I was about to blow my load in my jeans when I heard some commotion in the background down below me. I ignored whatever was going on down below and kept my eyes glued to her bed.

"Fuck, Drew, what the hell is taking you so long, man?"

I jumped back, almost falling off the roof as Zach came up the ladder. "Is everything okay?"

"Yeah, yeah. It's fine." I swallowed hard. I could feel my face going red as I scrambled to grab the next strand of lights. "I just needed to replace a few hooks that had rusted off on this window, but I need to get more for the others. Let me come down and grab some," I said, coming over to the edge of the roof, waiting for Zach to climb back down the ladder. The last thing I needed was him coming up on the roof with me and peeking and seeing what I witnessed.

Zach backed down the ladder, allowing me to come down. We fished around in the garage looking for more hooks, finally finding them tucked in Jim's toolbox. We both walked out of the garage, ribbing one another, and came around the corner. I stopped dead, dropping the package of hooks on the ground, as I saw Lexi standing on the porch talking with her father. She glanced over my way, waving.

"What the hell is wrong with you?" Zach asked, smacking me on the back. "Look like you've seen a ghost." He laughed.

"I'm fine." I shrugged, reaching down to pick up the package and heading for the ladder.

I sat in the corner of the coffee house reading the paper and sipping on hot coffee, trying to relax. After I had gone back up on the roof to finish the lights, Lexi had gone back into the house to bake with Barbara. I had never been more relieved. I could feel the tension within myself as she had stood talking with her father, both glancing over at me occasionally. I knew Zach sensed it too because he kept staring at me. After she had gone back inside, I had to ignore his constant questioning and nagging. I had finished putting the lights up, and then decided to head into town. Now here I sat, alone with nothing but my thoughts and this cup of coffee.

I had been sitting here reading the same article repeatedly for the last twenty minutes, thinking of what I had seen through Lexi's bedroom window. I dropped the paper down and stared out the window as shoppers bustled up and down the street, carrying bags, laughing and talking with their shopping partners. Everyone around me seemed happy, and here I was, once again caught up in my own feelings, only this time they had nothing to do with Laura. Going away this Christmas was supposed to be a good thing.

I let out a sigh. I had done no shopping yet, and I needed to get on it. Christmas was fast approaching and wasn't going to wait for me to make up my mind on when and if I should start shopping. I drank down the remainder of my coffee and left the little shop, stepping out into the cold and blowing snow, and wandered up the street.

I spent the remainder of the day in town, wandering in and out of the shops, accomplishing nothing. I slowly wandered up the street and turned into the driveway of the house. Zach was busy securing his skis to the hood of the car.

"Hey, man, going skiing with Ann Marie?" I asked, stopping to help him for a second.

"No, she is busy with her parents and little brother. I was hoping you would hit the slopes with me tonight. Lexi is moping around the house, and Mom and Dad just want to relax."

I glanced at my watch. It was only seven. Plenty of skiing hours left. I thought for a quick second. I could stay at the house praying I could ignore Lexi or I could ski with my best friend. "Little night skiing, sure thing. Let me just run inside and get changed."

"Sure thing. I'll just finish up here."

I ran up the front steps and into the house, kicking my shoes off and running upstairs to my room. I quickly changed, grabbed my ski pants and jacket, and stepped out into the hall just in time to see Lexi climb up the stairs with a mug of hot tea. She looked over at me like she was going to say something, which was soon replaced with a sad look on her face. She walked into her room, closing the door behind her. I was tempted to go and see her, but I needed so bad to distance myself from her right now that I couldn't be bothered. The sad look in her eyes was no doubt because of me, because I was already disappointing her. Just as I knew I would.

Zach and I drove down to the ski hill, and he waited patiently while I grabbed some skis, and then we bought our lift tickets and headed up the mountain. For the next few hours, the only thing on my mind was scenery as we cut up the fresh powder beneath our skis. My mind was free of everything by the time we had loaded the car back up.

"You up for a coffee?" Zach asked as he climbed into the front seat of the car, doing up his belt.

"Yeah, you know what, that sounds great."

We drove over to the little coffee shop, Zach parked the car, and we both hopped out and walked into the shop. Standing in line, I looked around at the faces that filled the place. It was almost my turn to order when I spotted Lexi sitting over in the corner with Ann Marie.

"Hey, I thought your woman was busy with family tonight?" I said to Zach, who was busy looking up at the board trying to decide what he wanted to eat.

He glanced over to where they were sitting and smiled as he waved at her. "Guess she was all finished. Want to join them?"

My stomach sank as I noticed Lexi wipe tears from her cheek and get up from where she was sitting and go into the women's washroom.

"I guess," I said, frowning after her as I placed my order.

As we stood waiting for our order, Zach watched as Lexi came out of the washroom, eyes red as she looked over toward me and rushed back over to where they were sitting. While Zach and I continued to wait for our coffees, he bumped me with his shoulder and leaned into me. "You better not have hurt her," he said in a hushed tone.

My gut churned as I was handed my coffee cup. "You know, I'm suddenly not feeling all that well. Think I might head back to the house," I said, clearing my throat and looking back over at Lexi as she stared back to me.

"What the fuck, man, you were fine five minutes ago."

I didn't have much to say to that. I just couldn't be here in the same room with Lexi and her brother. "Think you could catch a ride with Ann Marie?" I asked, practically begging for the keys.

"I guess." He shrugged, pulling the keys from his pocket.

"Thanks, man. I'll see you tomorrow." I took the key from his hand, had my coffee put into a to-go cup, and quickly made my way over to the car.

I made it back to the house in no time and went straight to my room, locking the door behind me. I quickly changed and dropped into bed and flipped the TV on and spent the night alone with my thoughts.

The remainder of the week I spent my time in town

or with Zach. Every night, by the time dinner was over, I hit my pillow and it was all I could do not to slip across the hall and into Lexi's room. The way Lexi and I looked at one another through dinner or in quiet moments was beginning to weaken whatever strength I still had to stay away from her.

On Thursday night, once I retired to my room, I actually started locking my door. I wasn't sure if I was doing it to keep her from sneaking in throughout the night or to keep me from sneaking out.

Saturday morning, I woke early and stepped out of my room a little after five in the morning to use the washroom. Half asleep, I trudged across the hall and was just about to open the bathroom door when Lexi came out of the room wrapped in nothing but a thin white towel. My eyes dropped down her body as she scurried by me. It was impossible not to watch as she ran back to her room, and it took every fiber of my being not to follow her back into the bedroom, lock her door, and fuck her up against the wall, especially when she turned and practically begged me with her eyes to do just that.

Sunday morning, I joined everyone for breakfast for the first time in a week. I took my usual spot beside Lexi. Zach hadn't come up yet from the basement, Jim was out in the garage getting something out of the freezer, and Barbara had her back turned to the table plating up food. I picked up my coffee mug and took a sip, and that was when I felt a slight tug on my shirt sleeve.

"Why are you ignoring me?" Lexi whispered.

I put my mug down on the table and looked at her, so badly wanting to kiss her and make her worries disappear. I knew that I was getting to her. Hell, I was getting to myself. She tugged at my heart as her sad eyes looked up at me.

"Did I do something wrong?"

How could I answer that? She had done nothing, nothing at all. It was all me and my inner demons. "I'm not. I've just had a lot of things to do for work over the last few days," I lied.

Her eyes fell from mine down to the plate in front of her. "But you locked your door last night," she whispered.

I didn't have an answer for her, and as her sad eyes looked down away from mine and looked to her plate, I knew me staying away from her was hurting her far more than I really knew.

Alexa

"So what did you want to get for Drew?" my mother asked as we walked through the craft store.

"Nothing," I whispered, picking up a book on how to knit.

"Alexa! That is not the way we treat members of the family."

Says who? I thought to myself. That is how we treat members of the family who treat members of the family the way he had been treating me lately.

"Now, what do you want to get for Drew?"

"I'll probably just get him a pass for skiing on boxing day." I sighed, grabbing a book on woodworking that I was sure my father would like and adding it to my pile.

"Are you sure everything is all right with you?" Mom asked, stopping to look at me as I wandered down the scrapbooking aisle looking for something for Ann Marie.

"For the hundredth time, yes. I am fine," I bit out just as my cell phone rang. I pulled it from my pocket and looked down at the screen. "I have to take this," I said, handing my mother the stack of items I had chosen.

I wandered outside and slipped into a doorway, out of the wind. "Hello."

"Alexa, it's Cameron. Listen, if you want your job back, I have an assignment for you."

I let out a laugh. "As if, Cameron. Are you sure you haven't dialed the wrong number?"

"Look, you're the only one I know who can actually do this assignment. It starts on the thirtieth."

"Listen, I'm not coming back for one assignment, Cameron."

"Lexi, please, you don't understand. I need you."

"Should have thought about that before. I have to go. I'm out with my mother." I took a breath as I hung up the phone. I had no idea what I was going to do after Christmas, but it felt good to tell him off. I smiled to myself and wandered back into the shop to find my mother.

"Lexi, come on. These cookies aren't going to bake themselves," Mom called from downstairs.

I put the items I had purchased away a wandered down the stairs. I had spent a better part of the afternoon texting back and forth with Cameron, silently wishing he would go away. The stress of him begging was getting to me.

I made my way into the kitchen only to find Mom there with all the ingredients pulled out, looking irritated. "All right, so did you want to make them or should I?" she asked.

I looked over everything, the thought of trying to bake overwhelming me, and I burst into tears.

"Alexa, what on earth?" she asked, coming around the counter and wrapping her arms around me. I clung to her like I had done when I had been a child. The stress of everything pouring out of me.

"You're right, Mom, everything is a mess," I blurted through tears.

"What's a mess?"

"I did something I shouldn't have. I made a mistake. That's why I came home."

"What did you do?"

I could feel my stomach start to turn. "Oh, Mama, about a year ago, I got involved with my boss, and he fired me after we didn't work out. Now he wants me to take a job with him again."

I felt her place her hand on the back of my head and stroke my hair, just like she used to do when I was little and upset.

"Alexa, life is full of mistakes. This isn't going to be the first, and it certainly won't be the last. What matters is that you learn from them."

"Yeah, but I can't find decent work, Mom. I have a shitty job doing crappy assignments that I used to do when I first started. It's nothing like what I was doing. It pays half of what I was making, and things are so tight," I said, pulling away and wiping my eyes.

"Is that the reason you came home and brought everything with you?"

I nodded my head. "I'm sorry I didn't tell you the truth. Just another way I let you down."

"Alexa, you, my dear, have not let me down. What did you end up telling him?"

"I told him no." I gripped the angel charm around

my neck and closed my eyes. The headache I already had was now coming on full strength.

"Can I be honest with you, Alexa?"

I nodded my head and opened my eyes to look at her. "I think that I would be more disappointed with you if you took the job he was offering, to be honest. I would rather see you stay in the current job you're in, no matter how easy it is to you, or have no job at all. You can always stay back home for a while and find something here, if you are truly unhappy. Don't sell yourself out because you feel you need to work away from home. Now what else is bothering you?"

"Nothing." Here I went again, lying. I wanted to scream out that I had feelings for the man staying across the hall from me. I wanted to tell her that I thought he was the one and that I was crushed that, after a wonderful night together, he wasn't speaking to me.

"Alexa, I know my children, dear. Don't lie to me."

I looked at Mom, knowing full well she knew there was more. The sound of the front door opening caused me to jump and look over my shoulder. Drew and Zach walked in carrying a couple of bags of groceries my Mom must have asked them to pick up. Zach came up the stairs first, Drew trailing behind. Mom was already occupied with Zach. Drew took one look at me and mouthed, "Are you all right?" I gave him a nod and turned my face away from him.

"What are you boys up to now?" she asked.

"Heading out to ski," Zach answered as he grabbed a glass of water. "Want to come, Lexi?"

"Lexi isn't feeling well. Has a headache. She is going to stay with me and bake."

"Oh, well, feel better there, sis."

"Dinner will be on about seven. Don't be late," Mom called after them as she began putting the items away that they had purchased.

While Zach ran down to his room, I watched Drew grab his gloves from the closet, and then leave the room to get his ski pants. I couldn't help but watch after him. Mom finally cleared her throat, turning my attention back to her.

"What else is going on, Alexa? What else is bothering you?"

"Nothing, Mom. Let's just get these cookies baked. I'll help, but I don't want to make them on my own," I said, turning my attention to her while thoughts of Drew ran through my mind.

Alexa

❧

I walked with my head down, concentrating on my feet kicking through the snow. Last night, I had called my new boss over in Europe and spoke with him about my upcoming assignments after Christmas. As he explained my assignments I felt as if I were brand new in the industry, and my heart became more unsettled than before. I was feeling so conflicted. I didn't know what I was going to do. Come January, I would more than likely be on a plane back to Europe. Drew had barely spoken to me all week, and every time I had suggested we do something, he would come up with some excuse as to why he couldn't. I didn't know what I had done wrong, but when I went to talk to him about it the other night after everyone was in bed, I had found his bedroom door locked again. I even softly knocked, but he didn't answer.

He had been right, that one night had changed everything between us, and the way he was acting was making me regret my decision to climb into that shower. There had never been a time in my life that I could remember Drew not being there for me.

I wandered into the ski shop and stood in line, patiently awaiting my turn at the counter. I listened to the conversations around me, the laughter, the two love birds behind me kissing and snuggling, and in an instant I felt utterly alone. I smiled to myself as he quietly told the woman he was with how much he loved her. The smile fell from my face as I wished that Drew was here with me and that it was my ear those words were being whispered to. I also secretly wished that if he had confessed how he felt, I would know exactly what to do about work in the new year.

Fifteen minutes later, with a new sense of sadness surrounding me, I left the ski shop. I had the annual boxing day skiing tickets in hand for Zach and Drew, and I stepped out the front door to continue my way to the next stop I needed to make. As soon as I stepped out the door, I saw Drew across the street. He walked with his head down, his hands shoved into his pockets, and he stopped in front of Gwen's Book Shop and entered.

Excitedly, I went to step forward and collided with a man carrying bags upon bags of gifts, the force of him knocking me to the ground, and I fell with a hard thump.

"Watch where you are going, young lady," the man sneered as he continued walking without even stopping to see if I was okay.

"Yeah, Merry Christmas to you too, Scrooge!" I shouted after him as people around me looked down at me as I sat on the sidewalk.

Getting up, I brushed myself off and walked across the street to the bookstore. I peeked through the window and saw Drew speaking with the salesgirl behind the counter. He laughed at whatever it was that she said, and then he wandered off to the back of the bookstore. I let out a breath and pulled on the door, the jingling bell alerting my arrival. I smiled to the girl behind the counter and went off in the same direction as Drew.

I watched from a distance as Drew slipped into the History section. I quickly made my way up to where he was and slipped down the aisle in front of him. He had his back to me so I peeked through the shelves. I watched as he picked up book after book, reading the backs of them. I was enjoying the view of his ass in his snug jeans when he suddenly turned around.

I dropped to the floor, praying that he hadn't seen me, but it was too late. I heard him start to laugh on the other side of the shelf, and the next thing I knew, his feet were in front of me.

"Lexi? What are you doing?"

"Ah, there it is. I finally I found it," I said, grabbing a book from the bottom of the shelf without reading the title and standing up. "Thank goodness they have it and the girl was right, exactly where she said it would be!" I exclaimed. "I was afraid I would have to order it online and risk it not being here Christmas morning." I smiled.

I could feel his stare and peeked up at him, a soft smile resting on his lips. I could feel my cheeks start to burn as we stood across from one another. "Are you following me?" he asked, reaching and taking the book from my hand. He read the title and looked back up at me.

"No, no, I came in to get my mother this book for Christmas," I stated matter of fact.

"Is that so?" he asked, crossing his right foot over the left and leaning up against the bookshelf.

"Yes." I nodded. "You see she has been going on and on about that book. Even made the comment to me the other day while we were out shopping how badly she wanted it."

"Hmm, I see." He looked down at the cover of the

book again and smirked. "You sure she wanted this book? It just doesn't seem like your mother to me."

"What do you mean?" I asked.

"Well, I think it's awesome that you are out getting Christmas gifts, but for some reason I am sort of shocked that your mother would tell you she wanted a copy of *The Complete Illustrated Guide of the Kama Sutra.* I mean that is just something you would buy on your own," he said, turning the book around for me to the see the cover, a smile coming to his face.

I could feel my face heat as the embarrassment coursed through me. I had grabbed a book without even realizing what section I was standing in. I pulled the book from his hand and placed it back on the shelf, clearing my throat.

"What are you really doing here?" he questioned, still smirking.

"Fine, I saw you come in here. I..." A smirk settled on his face again, and I suddenly wished the words would fall from my lips instead of leaving me standing here looking foolish.

"So, you followed me?"

"Hardly. You've barely spoken to me all week! Barely even looked at me!" I hissed. Drew didn't say anything; he just stood there taking me in. "Was I just some kind of toy you thought you could use?"

"Lexi, come on, don't think that."

"What am I supposed to think, Drew? I went to come over to your room the other night and the door was locked. You've avoided even looking in my direction at dinner." I could feel the wave of hurt coursing through me.

"It was wrong, I know."

"Do me a favor and tell me now if I am nothing more than a fling for you. I need to know," I said, crossing my arms over my chest. It was the same defense mechanism I had used my entire life. If I crossed my arms over my heart, nothing would or could penetrate. However, I knew I had already lost that battle because with him he had already penetrated.

He stood staring back at me. "You aren't a fling for me, Lexi. I just needed to get a grip on my feelings."

I stared at him, taking in the expression on his face. I knew he wasn't lying, and his answer was enough for me to accept. I had feelings too; I just couldn't tell him how intense mine were or else he would run again, and I didn't want that. He was finally speaking to me.

"I think that right now we should keep this between us, okay?" He brushed the loose strand of hair that was in my face behind my ear and cupped my cheek.

I nodded, relishing the feel of his warm hand

against my skin. I closed my eyes, thinking to myself that he might be right. Until we knew what direction, if there was one, we were heading in, it would be best not to involve others. I had to be careful; I didn't want him to know how I felt right now, and I didn't want him to know that I was in love with him. I didn't want him to run again.

I looked down at my feet and back up at him, and he shocked me by slowly leaning in and brushing his lips against mine.

"Who is coming to church with us tonight?" Mom asked as she brought over the apple pie she and I had baked fresh this afternoon.

"I think we might join you, Mom," Zach said, putting his arm around Ann Marie and pulling her chair closer to him.

"All right. What about you, Drew?"

"Nah, I think I might just stay here. I have a few things I have to get done for the office," he said, taking the carafe of coffee from Dad and pouring himself and me a cup. Just as he set the carafe down, his cell phone rang. "Speak of the devil," he mumbled, grabbing it from his breast pocket. He looked at the screen and quickly excused himself from the table.

"What about you, sweetie?" my mom asked, pulling my attention away from Drew's backside. "I think it might be good for you to go."

I fiddled with the angel on the chain of my necklace while spooning some sugar into my coffee. "I don't think so, Mom. How about I stay back and clean up this mess for you instead."

She let out a sigh as she dished out the pie and passed a plate to each person around the table. "Are you sure, Lexi?"

"Positive."

Afterward, everyone went their separate ways to get ready for church, while I stayed in the kitchen getting things organized for cleanup. I had just run a hot sink full of water when I heard Mom clear her throat behind me.

"Lexi, a man called for you today. He told me to tell you that he would hold the apartment until you called him, but he can't hold it much past the first."

I turned and looked at her and could see the questions in her eyes before she even asked them. "What else is going on, Alexa?"

Chewing the inside of my cheek, I debated making something up to tell her but decided against it. "I don't know, Mom. I am just so up in the air about...everything!"

"I see." She came around the counter and crossed her arms.

"Aside from the job, it's just so lonely, Mom."

"This wouldn't happen to have anything to do with Drew would it?" she whispered.

I let out a nervous laugh. "No, why would you think that?"

She looked at me as if she knew what I was hiding. "I've seen the way you look at him, Alexa, and I know my daughter."

"Well, you are wrong, Mom," I said, busying myself with the dishes. She didn't say anything, but I could still feel her standing there looking at me. I turned around to face her.

"It's okay, Lexi," she said, pulling me in for a hug. "Things will come together, don't you worry. Are you sure you wouldn't rather come to church with us?"

I looked around the kitchen at the mess before me and thought of Drew upstairs. "Yeah, it's okay."

I took the message my mother had written down

and hung it on the fridge to deal with after they left. I watched as she made her way to the front door where everyone was waiting for her.

"Have fun!" I shouted.

The house was finally quiet. Mom and Dad had retired to their room with two hot mugs of tea the minute they had gotten home from church. Zach and Ann Marie had sat in the living room for a while before doing the same, leaving me alone upstairs. I had made a cup of peppermint tea and curled up in front of the Christmas tree, a warm fire burning.

I turned on the radio, Christmas music filled the room, and I watched the soft glow of lights dancing on the tree. I had so much to try and figure out in such a short time. It felt like time was really against me this year. I fiddled with the piece of paper that Mom had given me earlier, trying to figure out what to tell my landlord.

I jumped when I heard someone clear their throat. Drew stood against the bottom of the stairs in nothing but a pair of house pants, watching me intently. I hadn't heard or seen him come down the stairs and had no idea how long he had been standing there watching me. I softly smiled at him as he walked over and sat down next to me. I could already feel the heat radiating off him.

"Hey." I swallowed hard, taking in his muscular chest.

"What are you thinking about?" he asked, putting his arm around me and pulling me into him.

"Not too much," I said, letting my body adjust against his and closing my eyes as I rested my head against his shoulder and breathed in his scent. I had hoped that staying home tonight, Drew and I would have spent some time together, but he had stayed up in his bedroom until now. This was the first time in a week that we had been this close, and my body was already humming with excitement.

"You know what, I think you are lying." he said, bopping me on the tip of my nose with his forefinger. He had always had a way of reading me like no one other than my mother could.

I smiled. "No, not lying. Just trying to figure some things out is all. Did you want a tea?" I asked.

"That sounds good."

When I returned to the living room, Drew had placed a large blanket down on the carpet in front of the fireplace. He had pulled the pillows from the couch and scattered them around as well. He was sitting with his knees pulled up to his chest, his arms wrapped around them, staring into the fire.

"Here you go," I said, handing him the mug and sitting down cross-legged beside him.

We both sat in silence for a while, watching the flames of the fire dance, until I finally broke the silence. "So what are you still doing up? I figured you went to bed ages ago," I murmured, looking at the dancing orange and red flames of the fire.

"Like you, I too have things on my mind." He sighed, taking a sip of his tea now that it had cooled down.

We were both quiet again. I wanted to tell him how I felt—I so did—but I was so afraid that he would run again that I couldn't. However, the longer we sat in silence, the stronger that feeling stirred in my gut.

"Anything you care to talk about?"

He shook his head. I flopped back onto the floor, stretched my arms over my head, and let out a yawn. I stared up at the ceiling for a while, and when I finally decided to look over at Drew, I was surprised to find that he was watching me, his eyes dancing over my body.

Without saying a word, he rolled onto his side and,

keeping eye contact with me, lifted my shirt, exposing my stomach, and then he bent ever so slowly and pressed his lips to my bare belly.

I closed my eyes at the feel of his lips on me, finally opening them again when he pulled his lips away and found him once again staring into my eyes. I softly smiled and ran my fingers through his hair, while he continued placing tiny kisses along my tummy. He went inch by inch, lifting my shirt as he went. I felt that familiar ache stir at my center, and when he kissed the underside of my bare breasts, I squeezed my thighs tight together. He made his way to my neck, and then he finally met my mouth, his tongue sweeping across mine. His kiss was so deep, I could feel the want behind it as he wrapped me tightly in his arms, his strong, warm hand squeezing my waist.

"Take me upstairs," I murmured as he pulled away and studied my eyes.

Within minutes of asking him that, we fixed the living room and I was in his arms as he carried me up the stairs. He walked over to his room and shut the door behind us after placing me down on the floor. As soon as the door was locked, he walked over to me and reached for the drawstring on my pajama pants, tugging at it gently until the tie gave way, slipping them off me and letting them drop to the floor. Then he gripped the edge of my shirt, lifting it over my head and again dropping it to the floor as well, leaning in to bite my already hardened nipples.

I pushed at the waistband of his house pants, pushing them down over his hips. He kissed me hard, backing me up against the edge of his bed, where I sat down and took him in my hands, slowly stroking his beautiful, hard cock.

As I looked up, I noticed he was watching me intently as he ran his fingers through my hair. I bent and licked the bead of precum from the tip of his cock, listening to him inhale deeply as I swirled my tongue around him.

"Fuck, Lexi," he hissed, pushing me back onto the bed, until I was lying down looking up at him. He kneeled between my legs, forcing them open with his knees. I ran my hands over his hard abs, biting my bottom lip as I wished he were inside of me. With his knees holding my legs open, he looked into my eyes as he ran his fingers through my wet center, causing a chill to run through my body and my nipples to harden as his fingers found my clit. He supported himself with one arm and his mouth met mine to silence the moan that was about to come from my mouth as he continued to run his fingers over the already swollen bundle of nerves.

"You have to be quiet," he whispered as he continued teasing me.

"I can't," I whispered, "it feels too good.",

He pulled his hand away and reached over inside the bedside table, pulling a condom out. I heard the foil rip and opened my eyes to watch him roll it on. He bent down and licked each of my nipples, then kissed me deeply as I felt him press against my opening, finally slipping inside of me, filling me. He held me close as he pumped slowly and deeply inside of me, kissing me to stifle my moans.

Drew

The soft morning light peeked through the blinds, causing me to wake. I stared up at the ceiling, remembering last night. The feel of her soft skin against mine, her harsh breathing in my ear, and the little whimper she expelled as she finally came. I went to roll over and felt an arm around my waist, and panic started to rise. I glanced over at the clock and saw it was close to five.

"Lexi, baby, wake up," I whispered, gently shaking her shoulder. She didn't wake. Instead she readjusted herself and snuggled up closer against me. "Lexi, wake up," I once again said as I shook her. "You've got to get up, baby."

"Just go back to sleep." She ran her fingers over my chest.

"Lexi, come on, baby, your parents are home. Get up."

Her eyes opened abruptly, finally remembering where she was. "Oh my God, what time is it?" she asked, panicked as she looked around for her shirt.

"It's just before five."

I watched as she jumped from the warmth of my bed, the heat of her body leaving me, and threw on her pajama pants and T-shirt. She was just about to grab the door handle when we heard a door open on the other side, followed by her mother's voice speaking with her father. I could see the rapid rise and fall of her chest as panic set in, and I jumped up and went to her.

"It's okay, Lexi," I whispered. "Just stay quiet."

I could see the worry lining her eyes as she stood quietly in my arms, waiting for her parents to either go downstairs or back to bed.

"My God my bedroom door is open. I've never slept with it open." The panic rose in her once again as I rubbed her arms.

I had to do something to calm her down, so I grabbed my sweatpants and threw them on. "Give me a minute. You wait right here."

She looked at me as if I had lost my mind.

I pushed her behind the door and stepped out into the hall, pulling my door shut. Lexi's parents' bedroom door stood wide open, and I could see Jim facing the other way looking out the window. The bathroom door was shut tight, and I could hear the shower already running, which meant Barbara was in there. I slipped across the hall and pulled Lexi's bedroom door shut tight and was just about back to my room when I heard Jim clear his throat.

"Well, you're up bright and early. Merry Christmas, son!"

"Merry Christmas, Jim. I take it Barbara is in the shower?" I asked.

"Yep. She wanted to get breakfast prepared early so we can all make it to church on time."

"No problem. I'll just wait in my room." I went to turn to go back in when I heard Jim clear his throat.

"Oh geez, Drew, were you able to get that closet door open to put your belongings away? I forgot all about how it sticks."

"No, sir, but it's all right. I don't really need it."

"Nonsense, let me take a quick look," he said, starting to make way for my bedroom door.

"Jim, really, it's all right. Zach said he was going to help me with it later," I said, gripping his arm and looking him directly in the eye. "Really, it's fine." I could imagine Lexi freaking out behind the bedroom door at the thought of her father bursting inside.

"All right then, geez. I should go down and make some coffee. See you shortly."

I watched as Jim went downstairs, and then I went back into my room and shut the door behind me. "You're safe," I said, looking at an extremely panicked Lexi. I walked over to her and wrapped her tightly in my arms, kissing the top of her head as I felt her relax against me.

It was almost ten when we arrived at the church for the Christmas day service. We filed into the familiar old church that we had all grown up in, Lexi and I trailing behind everyone else. As she walked in front of me, I snuck a quick kiss on the side of her neck, praying that no one turned around to see it. We had spent such a wonderful night together, and having her wake up in my arms on Christmas morning had been the best gift I could have asked for.

Lexi slid into the pew and made enough room for me to sneak in beside her. Like always, she already had the hymn book in her hand and was marking out the music that would be sung during the service. She had always been like that, and I was glad to see she hadn't changed. I slipped my hand behind her and turned my body toward her. She looked up at me as if I had lost my mind. Putting my arm around her in front of everyone was apparently not allowed.

"What are you doing?" she mouthed at me, elbowing me in the ribs.

"What?" I shrugged my shoulders and winked at her. "Can't I put my arms around you?"

She ignored me and went back to searching through the hymn book. I looked over at the rest of the family. Ann Marie was talking with Barbara and Jim, and Zach was firmly engrossed in their conversation. No one was even paying attention to us.

I leaned down so my mouth aligned with her ear. "No one is even paying attention, watch. Don't make a sound." I kissed her ear, sucking her earlobe into my mouth.

Her cheeks flamed red as she tried to hold her composure while squirming in her seat.

"I can't wait to slide into your tight pussy later on," I whispered. I was sure I was going to go to hell after saying this in church.

"Isn't that right, Drew?" I jumped up when I heard my name called and looked over to see Zach staring at us.

"What's that, man?" I asked, swallowing hard.

"Skiing tomorrow? Are we on?"

"Yeah, yeah, of course, we are on. Can't wait." Ann Marie looked at me and then to Zach and back to me again, a knowing smile on her lips as she looked to a very red-faced Lexi.

Fuck, I'd been caught.

I dropped my arm from behind Lexi and sat facing forward, putting on my good boy hat. Thankfully, the sermon began, and everyone's attention was finally off me. Now I just needed to make it through the next couple of hours trying to calm the raging bulge that was in my pants.

We had just returned to the house and were sitting in the family room sharing stories with Ann Marie from Christmas past when my cell phone rang. Lexi looked up at me and frowned as I looked at the screen.

"Can you guys excuse me for a moment?" I asked, frowning at what I saw on the screen.

"Sure thing. Don't be long. Gift exchange is coming up!" Zach said, getting up to refill everyone's apple cider.

I ran up the stairs, the vibration of my cell phone stopping as I picked it up. "Hello."

"Merry Christmas, Drew."

I felt my heart start beating hard in my chest at the sound of the voice on the end of the other line.

"It's Laura."

I had barely thought of her since I had been here, which had been a welcomed change from before. I swallowed hard as I wondered to myself about what the hell she wanted.

"Is this a bad time?"

"Do you think there could possibly be a good time?" I chuckled, my asshole side coming out.

"I suppose I deserve that."

"What do you want?" I couldn't help being abrupt but hearing her voice had brought everything back to me.

"Well, it's just that I am in the area visiting my parents and was hoping to maybe see you. I was hoping we could talk."

I pondered this for a minute. As much as I didn't want to see her, I also wanted answers. I deserved answers. After all, that was what I had come to seek, and truthfully, the only place I would get them was from her. I glanced down at my watch and mentally calculated the time it would take for gift exchange and dinner.

"All right, tonight at eight?"

"Perfect. Swing by my parents' place. I'll see you then. Oh and, Drew, Merry Christmas."

We had done our gift exchange shortly before dinner. Zach and Ann Marie had left with Joe and Barbara shortly after dinner to head to her family's for the evening, leaving Lexi and I at home. "I'll be back shortly," I called up the stairs to her.

"Okay, if I'm not here when you get back just come downtown. I may go out and snap some photos of the town square," she called down to me not even questioning where I was headed.

"All right," I answered. I grabbed my coat from the hall closet and headed out the front door. Lexi and I had promised to exchange gifts tonight after the family was in bed. I hurried down the porch steps and made my way to Laura's parents' place about twenty minutes away.

I rounded the corner thinking about Lexi when I looked up and saw the house off in the distance, and everything came rushing back, thoughts of Lexi leaving my mind. I walked slowly up the front steps to the front door and knocked, waiting to be let in. It was a cold night, a few clouds in the sky, but mostly the stars twinkled brightly above my head.

It was only a matter of seconds before I watched Laura come around the corner, smiling as she approached the door. She looked good, dressed in black dress pants and a white silk blouse with a red scarf around her neck. She pulled the door open.

"Hey." She smiled at me. "Come on in," she said, stepping off to the side.

I could hear her family chattering and laughing in the background as I stepped inside the foyer.

"It's good to see you." She grinned as she held her hand out for my jacket.

I was hesitant. She had said she wanted to talk, and I had assumed she meant in private, but I slipped my jacket off anyway and toed off my shoes.

She hung my jacket in the closet and then turned to me, smiling as she placed her hands on her thighs and looked around as if she didn't know what to do. Laughter erupted from the kitchen, and she turned and made her way back to where she had been.

"Drew's here," she called out as I followed behind

her into the kitchen where everyone sat around the kitchen table, dessert plates in front of them.

"Hi, Drew, it's great to see you," Laura's mom said, getting up from her chair and embracing me in a tight hug.

It was almost as if Laura hadn't run off with another man only minutes before we were supposed to get married, leaving me at the alter looking like an idiot. Laura patted the empty chair beside her, signaling me to sit down.

At first, it was awkward being back there with her family, and then I got into a debate with her father, and soon an hour had passed by. I glanced down at my watch, seeing that it was close to ten. I didn't want to be here all night. She had wanted to talk to me, after all. I leaned over and placed my hand on her knee. "Can I speak to you alone?" I whispered as everyone looked over at us.

"Of course." She smiled awkwardly, excusing us from the table, and got up. "Guy's we are just going to head out for a walk."

"Drew, it was great to see you again," her mother said, hugging me once again.

I walked out to the foyer and slipped into my shoes and grabbed my coat off the handle of the closet door.

"How about we walk down to the little cafe in town?" she murmured as she put her coat on.

"Sure. That's fine," I said, opening the front door and stepping out into the cold.

We walked in silence for a while through the brightly lit neighborhood, taking in the Christmas lights. It wasn't a comfortable silence by any means, and I struggled to find words to say to fill that silence while we walked. I had never been as glad to see the lights of the cafe as I was in this moment. As I approached the door, I was surprised to find the cafe open, not really thinking about the fact that it was Christmas day.

I opened the door and allowed Laura to step in front of me. She walked over to the seat beside the fireplace and unwrapped her scarf. "What would you like?" I asked.

"A coffee please," she said, sitting down and running her fingers through her hair.

I brought over two coffees and sat down beside her. She sat there looking at me, a smile on her lips, just like nothing had even happened between us.

"So you wanted to talk," I said, grabbing a creamer out of the bowl in front of me and pouring it into my coffee, followed by sugar. I wasn't wasting time.

She took in a deep breath. "Drew, I want to apologize."

"For?"

"The way things went down. I know it's all my fault."

I could barely believe what I was hearing. Of course, it was her fault.

"What happened?" I asked, placing the spoon down on the table.

She looked at me through tears as she stirred her coffee. She had more to say, I knew it. "I don't know. I guess I choked. About a month before our wedding, I met someone, and he brought something out in me that I couldn't fight. I didn't know how to tell you. I didn't really even think much of it at first, but then something changed."

"So, you just ran off? Just threw away everything that we had?"

"I figured it may not hurt as much that way."

I chuckled to myself. "Laura, just don't." I shook my head, taking a drink of the coffee I barely even wanted to drink now.

"He was different from you. He was adventurous and wanted to have fun, he wanted to see the world...and he wasn't you," she mumbled.

"Of course, he wasn't me," I said. "And where is the wonderful man now?"

"He left me about three months ago. We had gotten engaged, and then he came home one night and told me he had met some other girl one night in a bar we had been in. I tried to keep him, but he took off with her." She sniffled and wiped the tears from her eyes.

I glared at her, at the terrible display of emotion she was trying to trick me with. I cleared my throat and sat back in my chair. "So now you know how it feels. Doesn't feel so good, does it?" I spat, my angry, vindictive side coming out.

She pulled her chair closer to me and put her hands on my knees. "I made a mistake, Drew. I didn't realize how lucky I was to have you...until you were gone."

"Laura..."

"No, Drew, please just hear me out. I want us to have another chance. I want you back." She didn't give me time to even digest her words. Instead, she just leaned in and kissed me.

Alexa

I grabbed my camera from my bag and headed out the front door and down the road, the sound of snow crunching under my feet. I couldn't stop thinking about last night. After we'd had sex, we'd laid in Drew's bed, his arms wrapped tightly around me, and talked about anything and everything. Occasionally, Drew would whisper into my ear, and then we would kiss for a bit, and then continue talking. We then made love again for the second time, and afterward he'd laid behind me, wrapping his body together with mine, and I had dozed off in his arms. It had been perfect.

Off in the distance, two kids playing in the snow under the streetlights caught my attention, and I stopped to take a couple of pictures. A few more steps down the road, and I snagged a photograph of a young couple sitting on a park bench, his arms wrapped tightly around her. All the answers I had been searching for had seemed to fall into place for me last night, and today I knew, because all day today I had felt so at ease. I felt as if I were floating, as if a sense of peace had fallen around me and was protecting me from the cold, like a warm blanket. In those few hours with Drew last night, I knew for sure he was the one. I smiled to myself at the thought.

I continued my way downtown, stopping along the way to take pictures of anything I thought was worthy of one. The snow had started to fall halfway into town, big, large, wet flakes, and I pulled my hood up over my head while I continued my walk. I rounded the corner, and the little cafe that Drew and I had been in earlier in the week came into view. The memory of the hot chocolate I had there popped into my mind, and I decided I would head over and order one, text Drew, and wait for him there.

I was just about to the door when I looked through the front window and stopped in my tracks. I took a deep breath, fighting the large, aching lump in my throat as I tried hard to process what it was I saw in front of me. As Drew's words from last night floated into my mind, I watched him kissing Laura in the front window of our little cafe.

I felt my camera begin to slip through my fingers as I stood there watching as my heart broke. My camera hit the ground with a *thud*, not even the sound able to pull my gaze away from what was before me.

Tears burned in my eyes seeing him with her. A car horn blared, tearing my attention away from my shattered dream. I bent and picked up my camera, brushing it off and spinning around so they were out of my sight, and I began the long, lonely walk back home.

The tears continued to pour down my face, leaving cold trails of wet as the wind whipped around me. Then it was as if someone had thrown a switch, and I suddenly couldn't understand why I was crying. It wasn't as if we were in a relationship or anything. We had never talked about anything permanent, but every time that thought ran through my mind, my chest ached with an emptiness I couldn't understand. It was as if someone were taking a large knife and plunging it repeatedly into a fresh wound.

When my parents' house finally came into view, I practically ran up the hill. I had never been so glad to see home as I was right now. I ran up the front steps and through the front door, kicking my boots off and dropping my jacket to the floor before running upstairs and into my bedroom. I dropped to my bed and cried until the tears no longer fell, and a suddenly a wave of panic washed over me.

I had to get out of here.

I jumped up off the bed and pulled my duffle bags out from the closet and began packing my things. I was frantically shoving half a drawer of clothing into one when I heard the front door open. The sound of Ann Marie and my mother's laugh carried up the stairs. I continued to shove handfuls of clothing into my bag and began ripping apart the remainder of the drawers, mindlessly shoving things inside. I was so engrossed in packing that I didn't hear my bedroom door open.

"Lexi." I heard a soft voice behind me, but I ignored it and continued packing. "Lexi, honey, what's wrong?"

I stopped mid-shove and looked down at the mess of my duffle bag when I felt my mother's hands on my upper arms. In an instant, everything came pouring out of me, sobs shaking my body so hard that I had no choice but to drop everything.

"Oh, Lexi. It's all right, sweetie." My mom quickly shut the door behind her and pulled me in for one of her comforting hugs. "Lexi, sweetheart, what happened?"

"What hasn't happened?" I cried.

"Talk to me, Lexi," she said, holding me close.

I reached for the tissues and wiped at my eyes. "It's Drew. I saw him tonight with Laura...kissing."

"All right."

"I'm... Since he got here, we've been..." The words wouldn't pass my lips, and my cheeks heated at the thought of what I was going to tell my mother.

"Do you love him, Lexi?"

I didn't answer her question. Instead, I buried my face in her shoulder as the tears started to pour again. "I just can't do this, Mom. I need to get out of here," I said, instantly stopping the crying and turning to resume my packing.

"Lexi." Mom grabbed my arm, but I pulled away from her touch. "Alexa, stop right now!" she gritted through clenched teeth. "Do you love him?"

I slowly nodded my head, embarrassed at how stupid I had been getting involved with him in the first place. I dropped the shirts that were in my hand and turned to face my mother.

"You can't assume things; you need to hear him out. Perhaps it isn't what you think."

"I know what I saw, Mom," I barked back.

"No, you think you know what you saw. Alexa, let me tell you something, and you can do what you want with this advice. You need to hear him out. What if he feels the same way for you? What if you don't give him the chance to let him explain to you what you saw and you just leave? What if you walking out on him breaks him completely? He has been hurt in the past by woman walking out on him. Not only by Laura, but his mother as well. I know Drew. I have known him his whole life, and I know he doesn't and never has entered any kind of intimate situation with a woman if he didn't feel there was something there. You need to remember that you are as important to him as the rest of this family, Alexa."

"But we haven't been intimate," I lied, trying to swallow the embarrassment I felt at saying those words to my mother.

"Lexi, one thing I am not is stupid. I've seen the way the two of you have been looking at one another. A person would have to be blind to not know that you are lying. Please give me just a little credit."

I locked eyes with my mother and thought for a moment. Mom made sense, but a large part of me was terrified that if I did hear him out and it didn't end in my favor that I would be ruined.

"And what if it was what I saw."

"Well, it's better to know where you stand than to leave now and wonder about it forever. Plus, I think it's best that you stay home here."

"What is that supposed to mean?"

"Just what I said. Lexi, you have been on the run for the past three years now, floating in and out of different chapters of your life. When things get tough, you pick up and you're on your way again. I noticed it started the day grandma passed away."

"No."

"Yes, it did. Grandma passed, and a week later, you were on a flight to Australia. You worked there for a bit, got involved with a surfer, and when that went south, you moved to Italy. You came home only once that year for thirty-six hours, and then you took off again. It's a pattern that you have. Just like now."

I looked at my mother and felt the tears building again. I remembered what I saw in that window tonight, and the urge to run was even greater than it had been before. "I can't stay, Mom. I can't bear to hear him say he wants her instead. Now please leave me in peace to pack my things."

Drew

I pulled away from Laura's lips and shook my head. "We're over, Laura," I said, placing my hands on her shoulders.

"Drew, please. Don't make a scene. Just hear me out."

"I have heard, and now there is nothing more for me to hear. We've been over for a long time," I said, reaching for my jacket.

"I'm sorry. I just think we deserve to give us another chance."

"There isn't an 'us' anymore, and it wasn't just the fact that you left me at the alter. The feelings that we had for one another left years ago. You know I wasn't even that upset that you didn't show up that day. What plagued me the most was *why* you didn't show."

Laura looked down to her hands and inhaled deeply. "I guess I was afraid I might be missing out on something. I mean, when I think about it, I have been with you since I was sixteen."

"And now..."

"Well, now I know I am not missing out on anything except for you. I want you back. I made a mistake."

"I'm sorry, Laura." I looked at her as she stood there with tears running down her cheeks. "I'm sorry, but I can't be what you want me to be. There's someone else."

"What? What do you mean?" She sniffled, a look of shock and anger on her face.

"Exactly what I said: there is someone else."

"Who?"

"Alexa." I threw my coat over my shoulders and quickly slipped my arms inside.

Laura let out a loud laugh. "Please, Drew, don't be ridiculous. You two cannot possibly have anything in common."

"I've got more in common with her than I ever did with you. I've got to go," I said, looking down at my watch. "I promised her I would be home early." Walking over to the door, the little bell announced my departure as I stepped out into the cold.

I couldn't deny my heart any longer, and now that I had gotten my answers, I knew Laura wasn't a part of it. The kiss we had just shared felt as if I were kissing my sister. It ignited nothing in me, unlike the kisses I had shared with Lexi. She ignited something in me that I didn't even know was there.

I glanced at my watch again; it was almost ten. I stood in the town square looking around. I couldn't go back empty-handed. The first thing my eyes landed on was the local jewelry store. I could see a soft light on in the front window and ran over, placing my hand up to the glass to see if I could see anyone inside. Sure enough, Mr. Richmond, the owner, sat in the chair behind the counter writing in his ledger book.

I banged on the glass, hoping he would look my way. Sure enough, he did, but he waved his hand to signal that he was closed. That didn't stop me. Instead, I continued banging on the glass until he finally got up and came to the front door. He looked around, probably to make sure I was alone and wasn't going to ambush him. Once he was sure, he unlocked the door, opening it only far enough to bark out at me, "Son, we are closed. Need I remind you that it is Christmas."

"I know, sir, but I beg you, please, just hear me out."

Mr. Richmond looked at me as if I had lost my mind. "All right."

"I need a ring."

"Great, good for you," he said, shutting the door, but I put my hand up, stopping him.

"No, sir, you don't understand. I need a ring, an engagement ring, tonight, before she's gone."

He looked at me and rolled his eyes, opening the door a little more to let me in. "You crazy kids, haven't you heard of shopping before Christmas?" he barked, locking the door behind me.

"Sir, please, if you would just show me to the engagement rings."

"They are over there where I was sitting."

I let him go first, walking over to the display cabinet and opening it with a key.

I stood looking over the tray at my options, finally settling on a one-carat heart-shaped diamond with white gold band. I stood waiting while the man began boxing the ring.

"So this girl, she must be pretty special to you if you're out here on Christmas."

"She is very special, and I wouldn't be here if it weren't for my ex-fiancée kissing me only a few moments ago."

Mr. Richmond looked at me as if I had lost my mind. "You crazy kids. Next time get your shopping done before Christmas day," he said, handing me the little white felt box that he had tied a red ribbon around. I passed him my credit card and waited while he ran it through his machine.

With the ring in my pocket, I began the walk home quickly, calling ahead to speak with Jim. I had to ask his permission before I got back to the house. I wanted Lexi to be surprised, but I also wanted to do things right. The phone rang twice before I heard Barbara's voice answer.

"Hey, Barbara, it's Drew. Is Jim there?" I asked, breathing hard into the phone.

"Drew? Are you okay?"

"I'm fine, just in a rush."

"Certainly. Let me grab him." It was a matter of seconds before I heard Jim come over the phone asking me if I was okay.

"I'm fine. Listen, this is important, and I know it's going to come out of left field, and I'll explain everything later, but I wanted to ask you for your permission. I want to ask Lexi to marry me."

Twenty minutes later, I was standing at the end of the driveway looking at the taillights of a cab. I frowned and felt my heart drop as the driver loaded four large duffel bags into the trunk of the car. I said nothing to the driver. Instead, I ran up the front steps and threw open the front door. I wanted my girl in my arms, and to say I was slightly panicking would be an understatement.

Jim and Barbara looked up from where they sat, tears in Barbara's eyes. Zach and Ann Marie stood by the fireplace, Zach meeting my gaze as I shut the front door.

"I told her not to pack, but she was insistent." Barbara said, shrugging her shoulders. "Even Ann Marie and Zach tried speaking with her," she said, wiping her nose with a balled-up tissue.

"Where is she?" I asked, shrugging my coat off and hanging it on the corner of the banister, kicking my wet shoes off.

"Upstairs. She said she had a phone call to make to her landlord and her boss," Ann Marie whispered, her eyes full of tears as well. She curled herself into Zach's side and buried her face in his shoulder.

My heart thudded in my chest. I couldn't lose her. I ran up the stairs and threw her bedroom door open. She jumped as the door banged against the wall and frowned at me as she continued speaking to someone on the other end of the line.

"That's right, I sent the down payment through e-transfer. I will send the remainder of the rent tomorrow afternoon via e-transfer as well. Great, okay, I guess I will see you in a couple of days then, and I will pay you the rest at that time." She hung up her phone and threw it down on her dresser.

"What's going on, Lex?" I asked, stepping into the bedroom and looking around at the now-empty space. "Where are you going?"

"Now isn't the time for this, Drew. I have to get ready to go. My cab is here to take me to the airport."

My heart sank. She picked up her purse and placed the strap across her shoulder and pocketed her phone.

"Lexi, please..."

"I have to go, Drew." She reached up and placed a kiss on my cheek, lingering there for a second. "I left your gift in your room. I hope you like it, and I wish you both all the best."

I couldn't find the words as every part of me ached. She slipped past me and walked down those stairs. I leaned against the doorframe unable to move, and when I heard the front door shut and saw the cab back out of the driveway from the upstairs window, my heart shattered into a million pieces. I slid down and sat on the floor, my arms resting on my knees.

I had no idea how long I had sat like that, but the next thing I heard was my name being called. "Drew...Drew?"

I blinked hard as Barbara came into view. She was kneeling beside me, a worried look on her face.

"She left." Those were the only words I could get out before the first of the tears slipped down my cheek. I felt utterly embarrassed. There had only been one other time in my life that I had cried, and that was when I was six, the day my mother had walked out on Dad and me.

Barbara wrapped her arms around me and pulled me against her, and then the tears just poured. "She can't be gone," I murmured through heavy sobs. "She didn't even give me a chance..."

"I know, sweetie. It will be okay. She will come to her senses, I promise you. Now Zach is downstairs and waiting out in the car. He's going to drive you to the airport to get her."

"I can't." I sniffled. "I can't take another rejection."

"You won't have to. I know my daughter."

I looked up at Barbara. She looked down on me with a soft smile on her lips and eyes full of tears.

"She loves you. I could see it on her face. Go, go get her." She leaned in and placed a kiss on the top of my head. She backed up and cupped my cheek. "Andrew, even though I already think of you as my son, I can't wait to have you marry my daughter."

Alexa

I ran down the front stairs of the house fighting the tears all the way. The look on Drew's face as I kissed him good-bye broke my heart. I didn't give him a chance to explain, because I think it would have killed me to hear the words that he was going to say. It would kill me to know that he had taken Laura back. So I did the only thing I knew: get into the cab and go. This life worked for me, as lonely as it was, and packing my things up was the only way I now had of protecting my heart.

As soon as I was in the safety of the back seat of the cab and had told the driver what gate to drop me at, the tears started to pour. I studied the landscape through watery eyes as we passed through town. The first intersection we came to was where Drew and I had shared our first kiss. I could almost see us standing on that corner, the snow falling around us as his lips met mine. I remembered the way his lips grazed mine, cautiously at first, and then hard and with purpose. I could feel his hand at the back of my head, as his fingers wound through my hair. I could still feel the warmth his body gave off on my cold skin that night.

I blinked hard and quickly shoved that memory to the back of my mind as the cab pulled away from the intersection where we had stood.

I really wished he had taken the other way out of town, that way I wouldn't have been subjected to this drive. He pulled up to the next light, just outside of the little cafe. I looked at the front window where we had sat and had our hot chocolate, where he had surprised me with a hot cup full of those mini marshmallows. We hadn't seen one another in a few years, and yet he still remembered.

As we started to move, the cab stopped in front of the other window of the cafe, the scene I had watched through that window just a couple of hours ago that had broken my heart in two. Seeing him kiss Laura had just about swallowed me whole. It was amazing to me how one building could hold such two different memories for me. I wiped the stray tear from my cheek as the cab began to move again. I needed to get out of this town.

I glanced out the window and to my left as the cab stopped at the next light, just in time to see the sign of the bookstore as the cab pulled away. My mind flashed to Drew's face as he looked at the book I had chosen to give my mother. That sexy half-smirk as he had caught me in my lie. The memory of him turning that book around to show me the title and how he had struggled not to laugh brought a soft smile to my lips.

I remembered that night as we made love in his bed, the feel of his hands caressing my body. The familiar scent of his cologne as he lay on top of me, gently pumping into me until I could no longer hold back. The way he held me as I came undone in his arms. The gentle caresses and kisses he had bestowed upon me afterward as he held me in his arms, never once letting me go. The sound of his sleep-filled voice as he whispered into my ear how beautiful I was.

"Do you think you could hurry up? The airport is bound to be busy tonight, and I don't want to miss my flight," I said to the cab driver through tears, as I felt my heart start to break again at the thought of not having Drew anymore.

He looked at me through his rear-view mirror,

concern lining his face, and passed me a handful of tissues over the seat. "Sure thing, miss. Are you okay?"

"Fine." I sniffled as I grabbed the tissues from his hand and sank into the back seat in time to feel my phone vibrate in my pocket. I pulled it from my pocket, almost afraid to look at the screen. Ann Marie's name sat on the screen.

Ann Marie: Lexi, you going to be okay?

I couldn't text her back right now. Was I going to be okay? Who knew? All I knew was my heart had just been shattered into a million pieces, and the farther I could get away from Drew and Denver, the better off I would be.

When we arrived at the airport, I pulled my bags from the trunk of the cab and handed the driver a handful of crumpled bills, while stacking my bags on one of the luggage carts. My body ached as I lifted the last of the heavy bags and wheeled the cart inside and wandered over to the check-in. My phone was still going off in my pocket, but I now chose to ignore whomever it was. The sooner I was on the other side of everything, the happier I would be.

Drew

I sat in the front seat of the car watching as Zach weaved in and out of traffic. We were both quiet as he concentrated on the road in front of us, coming to a halt as the car in front of us jammed on its brakes. Zach swore under his breath, coming just inches from rear-ending the guy in front of us.

"Thanks for doing this. I know you probably hate me right now."

"Drew, I don't hate you. You're like a fucking brother to me, man," Zach said, once again slamming the brakes on and laying on the horn. The guy in front of us flipped us the bird as Zach drove around him.

"I know. It's just you didn't seem too thrilled to see—"

"I was worried you were going to hurt her, man. I

was worried you weren't over everything with Laura is all. It's just an instinct for me to protect her."

"I've told you I'm over her, but no one seems to believe it." I chuckled.

"Well, I was wrong. Ann Marie kindly pointed that out to me, and basically I would have blue balls for the rest of my life if I didn't help you today."

"Ah, so you were bribed."

He chuckled again, slamming on his brakes and swearing under his breath at the car in front of us. "Something like that."

"You know, she's been out of my life for six months and she is still managing to fuck everything up for me," I said aloud as Zach started driving again.

"Not this time. I've seen our lives flash before our eyes more in the last five minutes than ever before, she isn't going to win. You, my friend, are getting Lex back!"

An ache in my gut started at the thought of holding her in my arms once again and smelling her vanilla-scented hair as she tucked her head under my chin and rested her cheek against my chest. I couldn't wait to hold her against me and kiss those beautiful, soft lips. I needed her in my arms more than I had ever needed someone before.

Zach finally pulled into a parking spot at the airport and we both jumped out of the car and ran into the building. We approached the checkout counter, pushing people who were waiting out of the way and making our way right to the front of the line. The lady behind the counter looked at us with disapproval as we stood on the other side of the counter.

"Gentlemen."

"Sorry, but it's an emergency. We are trying to find a passenger who may have already checked in."

I just happened to look up at the ticker board and saw the only flight to Italy was already in boarding status. I tugged on Zach's coat sleeve as he gave Lexi's name to the agent behind the counter.

"Forget it, man, we're too late. She's boarding." While the words fell from my lips, the agent behind the desk confirmed what I had just said.

Zach looked to me and then back to the agent. "You need to get her off that plane," he said sharply and forcefully to the agent behind the desk.

"Excuse me?"

"We've got a family emergency. You need to get her off the plane."

"Sir, her luggage has already been put on the plane."

"That doesn't matter. We will deal with that later. My sister needs to come home with us right now." Zach kept his cool while dealing with the agent and was relentless, until she finally succumbed and paged for Lexi to come to the main information booth at the front of the airport.

I stood off to the side with him and waited for what felt like forever, until I caught a glimpse of her dark-brown hair. She came running from the secured area and stopped dead in her tracks at the sight of both Zach and me.

"What the hell?" she demanded.

I went to approach her, but she held her hand up and started to back away, tears instantly streaming down her face.

"Alexa, just fucking listen. I didn't almost kill us to watch your stubborn ass get back on that plane," Zach called out from behind me, halting her in her tracks. He had never spoken to his sister that way.

I took a step forward, holding my hands out in front of me in a gesture of truce, finally getting close enough to grab hold of her hands.

"For the past week and a half, I have been trying to wrap my head around my growing feelings for you. I really wasn't sure how I should feel about you, especially after everything that I've gone through. Part of me wanted to be cold and detached, but that isn't who I am. Once the feelings really started, I became so afraid of them. I was mostly afraid of having my heart broken, but I was more afraid that I was going to let you down, partially because I couldn't understand why I was left at the alter. When Laura called today and asked me to come and meet her, I couldn't say no. It was my chance to find out why."

"You kissed her. I saw it all through the cafe window. It tore my heart out, Drew, seeing you with her after everything." Lexi sniffled and turned away from me.

I put my hand on her arm, praying that she would turn around and face me. When she finally did, my heart wasn't prepared for what I saw: her beautiful eyes watery with tears so up close and personal.

"No, you're wrong, she kissed me," I said, placing my hands on her hips and pulling her toward me. "I'm a lot of things, Lexi, but one thing I am not is a cheat. She left me for another man because she felt like she was missing out on something with me."

"But you are unsure of your feelings for me...you just said it."

"No, not anymore. I know how I feel about you. Yes, at first, I didn't want to ruin our friendship or turn out like my mother, a commitment-phobe. I was so afraid of letting you down because I felt that I had let one girl down, but now I know it was her own insecurities, not me, that caused her to run." I took her hand in mine and pulled it up to my mouth to kiss the back of it.

"I don't understand. You're afraid of those things, but how does this end with you locking lips with your ex?"

"As I told you, she kissed me, and if you had snooped just a little bit longer, you would have seen me pull away. You also would have seen me tell her to her face that she and I are over and that there is someone else. Someone that I am totally head over heels in love with. Then you would have seen me leave the cafe and run across the road to the jewelry store and buy this." I reached my hand into my pocket, producing the little white box.

Her eyes locked with mine, and for once Lexi was speechless. I dropped down on my knee in front of her and she looked down at me, shock and awe in her eyes.

"What...what are you doing?" she murmured.

I stood there blinking hard, his words washing over me as I tried hard to digest them. He was in love with me? He loved me. The realization of what he had just said hit me. "But, Drew, you went to see her."

"I went to see her for closure, nothing else. She's my past, Lexi, but I'm hoping that you will be my future."

I studied his eyes, as he held up a little white box wrapped neatly with a red ribbon, the look in his eyes saying everything. "I planned to do this a little bit later, and in private, but there doesn't appear to be much time, since you're planning on leaving the country."

"I don't think I will be. My plane and my luggage just took off."

"Well, I think I'll do it now anyways, before I lose

the nerve," he said as he looked around, and that was when I realized that the entire airport was watching us.

"Okay." I giggled, my cheeks heating in anticipation.

He quickly untied the ribbon and opened the box, holding it up to me. "I'm used to women walking out on me, Lex, and never turning back, but I'm really hoping that you will be the one woman that stays with me, forever and always. I love you, and I want nothing more than to spend the rest of my life with you."

I looked down into his blue eyes as he stared up at me with a look of want and hope. Through tears, I nodded as my hand went to my mouth to stop the sobs that were surely going to start if he didn't kiss me soon. He pulled the ring from the box and slipped it onto my finger and stood.

"No tears, Lex, unless they are happy ones."

"They are. They so are," I said, quickly wiping them away as he pulled me against him, devouring my mouth. In an instant, I was lost in his kiss, his hand cupping my cheek and his tongue making its way between my lips, sweeping through my mouth.

"Yes, yes, yes," I moaned into his mouth, his lips meeting mine again.

This time the airport erupted in loud claps as people cheered for us. I looked around, first in shock and awe, and then in deep embarrassment as the people continued to clap, some women even crying.

I wrapped my arms around Drew and hugged him tight and saw my brother standing there watching us, a soft smile on his lips as he held his phone up to his ear, surely speaking with Ann Marie.

"She said yes!" Drew shouted as we walked through the door.

"I knew it!" Mom said from where she sat on the couch. She got up and came over, wrapping her arms around me, and then Drew followed by Dad and Ann Marie.

"I just put a pot of coffee on and have some cinnamon rolls in the oven. This calls for a celebration," Mom called out, rushing into the kitchen.

"Welcome to the family, son," Dad said, smacking Drew on the back as he too followed Mom to the kitchen.

Ann Marie hugged me and then Drew before she disappeared with Zach into the kitchen, leaving us in the living room. I hung up my jacket in the closet and felt Drew slip his hands into my front pockets and kiss the back of my neck.

"Happy?" he murmured as he continued to trail kisses to the top of my shoulder.

"I am. Are you?"

"More than you'll ever know."

"All right, you two, break it up before I get sick," Zach said, coming down into the living.

Drew let out a laugh. "That so reminds me of the night of your junior prom, Lexi."

"You remember that?" I asked, somewhat shocked.

"How could I forget the first time I ever told you that you were beautiful." He leaned in and kissed me again.

"My God, man, you lay it on thick...Please stop." The three of us laughed, and we headed up to the kitchen to join the rest of the family.

Drew

2 months later

I was walking by my receptionist's desk on the way back to my office when Sophie stopped me. "I have a couple things I need you to sign before you leave for tonight."

"No problem, Hazel. Let me know when Sophie is back." I opened the door to my new office. The words "Junior Partner" never looked so good written under my name.

"Of course, Drew. Oh, and Alexa is on line one for you."

"Great, thank you." I pushed the door open and

grabbed the phone on my desk. "Hey, sexy," I purred into the receiver.

"Mom and Dad sold the house." Lexi's strained voice came over the line, and I could tell right away that she had been crying. "Set to close in two months." I heard the sniffle as she held back tears.

I got up and closed the door to my office and went and sat back in my chair, putting my feet up on the corner of my desk and loosening my tie. "I'm sorry, sweetie."

"It's not like I didn't know it was coming. It's just going to be hard to say good-bye, you know what I mean?"

"I do. Did you get the actual closing date? I mean, perhaps I can arrange to get some time off and we can go and spend a couple of weeks up at the house before the wedding."

"She sounded so upset, Drew, I didn't bother to ask. I'm assuming it is probably two months from today. She said she was going to go and call Zach next."

"I'll take a look at my schedule and see what I can do, okay."

"Okay. Are you going to be home soon?"

"I just have two things to wrap up, and then yes, I'll be home. How about we meet for dinner at Lorenzo's tonight?"

"That sounds wonderful. I just have this shoot to finish and I will be on my way."

Sophie walked into my office carrying some paperwork, and I held my finger up to signal that I just needed one second. She nodded and sat down across from me.

"Okay, sweetie, I've got to go. My last appointment just came in. I love you."

Her soft voice came over the phone. "I love you too. See you soon."

"Will do." Hanging up the phone, I looked to Sophie. "Everything good?"

"Yep, just need your signature on a couple more documents before I file them for finalization."

"Sounds good."

She passed me four documents all marked where she needed my signature. I signed quickly and handed them back to her.

"You're sure that is everything?"

"Yep, I'm sure. Give me a half an hour and I will have copies for you."

"Great, I'll be here." I smiled at her as she walked away.

As soon as she was out of the room, I leaned back in my chair and thought back to the phone call with Lexi, and how I had wanted to tell her my surprise but figured it would be better over a bottle of champagne tonight at our favorite restaurant, after she had already digested the news of her parents selling the house.

I did some paperwork and then called the restaurant to confirm our reservations and make sure that they had indeed brought in the bottle of champagne I had requested, since they didn't normally have it on the menu. It was a special favor from the owner to repay me, the newest partner in the law firm who had saved his restaurant from being taken over by his ex during the divorce.

I was seated at our favorite table in the back of the restaurant when I saw Lexi walk in. I patted my jacket pocket, making sure the documents were in there, when she spotted me and made her way over to our table.

"What made you choose Lorenzo's?" Lexi asked as she kissed me hello and sat down across from me.

"Just thought I would treat my girl," I said, winking at her.

"What a nice surprise."

Lexi flipped her menu open and started looking over the selections. I smiled to myself. She did this every time we came here but always ended up ordering the same thing. I signaled to the waitress who came right over.

"Sir."

"Can we get two glasses of water and a bottle of your 2009 Cristal Brut please." I immediately noticed Lexi's head snap up at the mention of the bottle of champagne.

"Are we celebrating something?" she asked, looking off into the distance, searching her mental calendar of important dates. "No, there is nothing that I can think of..."

"Relax. Can't I treat my girl?" I asked, trying to brush it off as nothing.

"Well, you can, but not with an eight-hundred-dollar bottle of champagne, Drew." She let out a nervous laugh and closed her menu.

"Just sit back and relax." I winked at her, placing my hand on hers, as she settled back into her seat.

"Please, Drew, just tell me. Is something wrong? Did you lose your job?" There was panic in her voice.

Just then the waitress showed up and poured us each a glass of champagne, setting the bottle in the center of the table. I kept eye contact with Lexi, watching the questions wander through her mind.

"Are you ready to order?"

I was just about to say yes when Lexi spoke up. "Could you give us a few minutes please?" Her eyes were still locked with mine.

"Of course." She nodded and quietly left the table.

"I can't eat until you tell me what is going on," she said, picking at her thumb, a nervous habit she still hadn't outgrown.

I let out a breath and looked at her, unable to decide whether I wanted to share it now or not, but I knew I had to. I reached into my jacket pocket, pulling out the first set of documents Sophie had given me, and passed them over to Lexi without saying anything. She reached across the table and took them from me, opening them as if they contained bad news. She looked them over, flipping between the pages, and then looked at me.

"I don't understand what these are."

"Well, the ones on the top are the sale of our house."

"What? What are you talking about? You sold our house without consulting me?" She was angry, her cheeks reddened, her body taking on a defensive posture.

"I did," I answered, straight-faced.

She stood up and grabbed her coat, throwing it around her shoulders. She grabbed her purse and began to walk out of the restaurant but then turned back, walking over to the table.

"How dare you do that, Andrew. How dare you." She whipped back around and took two steps forward, again stopping.

"Do you not even want to know why I did this?" I called out. I knew she was upset by the way she held her body as she stood there.

It was close to a minute before she finally turned toward me. "I'm curious."

I pulled another set of papers out of my pocket and held them out to her. She slowly stepped forward and removed the papers from the envelope, unfolding them. As soon as she began to read, her face relaxed, and then the tears started to pour. Her hand flew to her mouth. "Is this for real?"

"Yes, Lexi, it's real." I stood and stepped toward her waiting for her to realize I was telling her the truth.

Finally, she dropped the papers to the ground and crashed into me, wrapping her arms around my neck, kissing me passionately and thanking me profusely.

Epilogue

Alexa

Christmas

One Year Later

"Jingle Bells" played in the background as I stirred the bowl of cookie batter. I was getting frustrated because it looked nothing like my mother's.

"This should be dough by now," I murmured as I looked down to the bowl full of watery mess. "Why are you not working!" I screamed to the empty kitchen as I dumped the third bowl of ruined dough into the garbage. What the hell had I been thinking agreeing to host Christmas when we could have went to Hawaii and visited my parents?

I began again, starting in order of the ingredients on the card that I had carefully copied from my mother when the phone rang. I wiped my hands on my apron and picked up the phone. "Hello."

"There's my sexy wife. How's everything going? Everything okay at the house?"

I instantly smiled at the sound of Drew's deep, sexy voice. "Hey, baby, yeah, everything is fine. What time do you think you will be home?" I asked, looking down at the matching wedding band that now accompanied my diamond.

"Should be home around four. Traffic just opened up. It's getting busy in town with all the tourists."

"Great, I can't wait to see you." I giggled into the phone. "Oh, and just so you know, I'm not wearing any panties."

"Lex, you can't do that to me, babe. Play fair."

Drew had been gone for a week back to New York to finish cleaning out his office and tidying things up at the other law office. We had moved to Denver six months ago, after Drew had surprised me by selling his home and buying my parents' house in secret. The law firm he had been working for opened a branch out here, and Drew was handed the torch to lead this firm. I could still remember the night he presented the documents to me. I had gone through a whole range of emotion within ten minutes of arriving at that restaurant before I finally collapsed into his arms.

"Sorry, baby, but you know I don't play fair," I whispered and then giggled into the phone.

"Yeah, no kidding. Did you hear from your brother?"

"Yeah, he and Ann Marie will be here shortly."

"Great, and your parents?"

"They arrive tonight. Zach already said he and Ann Marie would pick them up from the airport."

"That would be great. Okay, sweetie, I'm off. I'll stop at the grocery store and pick up those items that you asked me to get before I get home. I guess I will see you shortly."

"I can't wait." I giggled into the receiver.

I hung up the phone and continued my venture of watching another damn recipe fail as I added the exact same measurements and ingredients into the bowl, which only resulted in the exact same mess I had before. Frustrated, I walked out of the kitchen and looked out the front window.

I had already re-arranged the furniture in preparation for Zach, Dad, and Drew to get the tree in the morning. I seriously couldn't wait to have everyone here in the house once again. I looked around and quickly straightened the blanket that lay across the back of the couch and fluffed up two of the pillows before wandering back into the kitchen to dump yet another messy mixture of what were to be cookies in the garbage. I placed everything into my new dishwasher we'd had installed and went upstairs to get changed before everyone arrived.

I had just stepped foot into our bedroom when my cell phone rang. I frowned, glancing down at the screen, a soft smile coming to my lips. *Finally*, I thought. I had been waiting patiently all day for this call.

Drew and I lay in bed. Everyone was all tucked in and probably asleep by now, after a long day of festivities. Surprisingly, my first Christmas dinner had turned out perfectly, with a little help from Mom, and after we had eaten we had gone downtown to the ski lodge. Zach, Drew, and Ann Marie took in the slopes, while Mom, Dad, and I sat in the lodge.

"Did you have a good Christmas?" Drew asked,

running his fingers through my hair as my head rested on his chest.

"I did. Even better knowing that you won't have to travel any longer for work." I kissed his shoulder and scooted over in the bed so my body was against his.

Drew had finally finalized everything at the firm he was at and had been given the go ahead to start hiring at this firm here. The first person he asked was Zach. He had agreed to join him in the new year. Ann Marie was so giddy with excitement that she started looking right away for a house in the area.

He pulled me in tighter yet, and I let out a large sigh. "What are you thinking about?"

"I just can't believe it's been a year. So much has changed. Last year at this time I had packed my bags and was getting ready to board a plane and never hear you out."

"Aren't you glad you got off that plane?" His lips grazed mine.

"I am. I so am."

"So am I." Drew shifted his body down beside mine and pulled me into him, allowing my head to rest flat on his shoulder as his hand cupped my cheek and he kissed me deeply.

"And now look. We are living in my parents' house,

you're about to open and lead a law firm, and my brother is going to join you."

"I know. It's somewhat unbelievable, to be honest."

"I agree." I rested my hand on his abs and let out a large yawn.

"And all because you got off that plane," Drew whispered, kissing me once again.

"Oh, I also wanted to talk to you about perhaps remodeling one of the spare bedrooms in the spring."

"Oh, sweetie, I don't need a home office. I won't be working like I was back in New York. There just won't be enough work, and if there is, I honestly don't need to bring it home with me."

"I wasn't thinking of an office."

"Oh, did you need something to do with photography? I mean we can always make the basement into a photo studio for you if you need. I mean you do have all the equipment. Perhaps a new backdrop would be something you would like. That way you can work from home."

"I wasn't thinking of that either, Drew."

"Well then, what would we remodel a room for?"

"A nursery," I said, propping myself up on my elbow and looking down into his eyes, a smile on my lips.

He studied my face, and I could see the beginnings of a smile on his lips. "For real, baby?"

"For real."

He rolled me over onto my back and met my lips, kissing me hard. "Two of the best Christmases in a row —the first one getting you, the second you are giving me the greatest gift I could ever ask for. I love you, Alexa. Merry Christmas, baby."

"Merry Christmas."

A Note from the Author

Dear Readers,

I would like to thank you for taking the time to read Back to You This Christmas. I hope you enjoyed Drew and Lexi's story. If you did, I would love it if you would drop me a review. Reviews are so important and really help me; I love to hear what my readers think.

I would really like to thank each of you who have supported me throughout the last couple of years. This journey has been amazing so far and I look forward to many more years of bringing you stories to get lost in.

About the Author

S.L. Sterling had been an avid reader since she was a child, often found getting lost in books. Today if she isn't writing or plotting, she can be found buried in a romance novel. S.L. Sterling lives with her husband and dog in Northern Ontario.

To learn more about me and my books visit my Website
https://www.authorslsterling.com

Want to keep in touch?

Sign up to receive my weekly newsletter

Or

Join my Reader Group
Sterlings Silver Sapphires